'Cold?'

Dan put an arm ⎯⎯⎯⎯⎯⎯⎯
shoulder against his.

'Mmm,' she said, her heart giving an unexpected lurch as she reluctantly felt the pull of his attraction. 'And thinking of the long walk back.' What on earth am I doing here…with him? she asked herself furiously. It was as though her mind and body had become split, and her body was responding to its own urgent needs, getting the better of her.

Again Dan sighed, putting his head back against the rough bark of the trunk, closing his eyes. Signy glanced at his profile, his face so close to hers.

Without moving, or opening his eyes, he said softly, 'Signy, I want to kiss you…I want to hold you in my arms.'

Rebecca Lang trained to be a State Registered Nurse in Kent, England, where she was born. Her main focus of interest became operating theatre work, and she gained extensive experience in all types of surgery on both sides of the Atlantic. Now living in Vancouver, Canada, she is married to a Canadian pathologist and has three children. When not writing Rebecca enjoys gardening, reading, theatre, exploring new places, and anything to do with the study of people.

Recent titles by the same author:

CHALLENGING
DR BLAKE

BY
REBECCA LANG

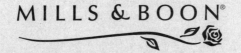

*First published in Great Britain 2002
Harlequin Mills & Boon Limited,
Eton House, 18-24 Paradise Road, Richmond, Surrey TW9 1SR*

© Rebecca Lang 2002

ISBN 0 263 83075 6

*Set in Times Roman 10½ on 12 pt.
03-0602-53061*

*Printed and bound in Spain
by Litografia Rosés, S.A., Barcelona*

CHAPTER ONE

THE first thing she really noticed about the man she had come to meet, after the initial quick assessment, was that he had a broken nose. That is, he had at one time had a broken nose. The second thing she noticed was that in spite of the nose—or perhaps because of it—he was attractive.

Signy Clover averted her gaze, shifted her attention away from the two men who stood a few yards away from her, intent on their conversation. The view was spectacular from where she stood outside the small, private air terminus building. It was here that the float planes took off from Vancouver to some local destinations, along the coastline and to the various islands off the coast.

In front of her was the wide sheltered bay that led out to the Pacific Ocean, while to her right, to the north, were the mountains, those belonging to the coastal range, not the Rockies, so she had read. Even though she was tired and jet-lagged, Signy felt a rare thrill as she looked at them. The feeling of pleasure came as a welcome surprise. For a while she had thought that she might never be able to experience any sort of joy again or, at least, not for a long time. Her time in Africa seemed to have squeezed all capacity for pleasure out of her.

Below those mountains, below the densely forested areas of the lower slopes, as well as behind her, were the high-rise buildings of the city. Slowly she looked around her, marvelling at everything that was so new to her. Over to her left, on the other side of the wide bay, were hills that were covered with pale houses and vegetation in various shades of green, small in the distance.

The air was very clear, with a limpid quality to it that made objects seem closer than they were, like the float plane that was coming across the bay to touch down in the water. It seemed to move on the breeze, not powered at all, as it came slowly downwards to the blue water, like a toy, glowing white in the sunshine. Signy felt as though she could reach out and touch it.

The climate wasn't always like this, so she had read in the training manual that had been sent to her before she had left England. Thick cloud could come down in a matter of moments, obscuring the mountains, the high-rise buildings of the downtown area, the freighters anchored out in the bay.

The two men appeared to be winding up their conversation, moving away from each other, so Signy's attention was brought back to them, particularly to the man she had come to meet, the one with the broken nose. After lifting a laconic arm in farewell to the other man, he turned his attention to her, walking over to her where she stood on an expanse of concrete, surrounded by her few pieces of luggage. A taxi had deposited her there minutes before.

'That's him over there,' the receptionist had informed her when she had enquired for Dan Blake at the squat, rather ramshackle terminus building with the flat roof. 'He's the tall one with the fair hair.' Since then she had waited for him to finish his conversation, knowing that he had seen her and was expecting her.

'You must be either Signy Glover,' he said, coming to a stop about two feet away from her, 'or Terri Carpenter. With World Aid Nurses?' He had a pleasant voice, low and slightly clipped, a mixture, she thought, of English and Canadian accents.

Close up he looked a little older than she had at first thought him to be. There were fine lines fanning out from the corners of his grey-blue eyes as he squinted at her against the sun, lines of tiredness and exposure to the elements, she thought. He spoke slightly out of the corner of his mouth, like an actor in a gangster movie or a Western—the bad guy. Not my type, she found herself thinking cynically as they appraised each other quickly. Just as well, because I don't want to get involved with any man, in any way, during this training and rest period. Dan Blake, she felt, was one man she could rule out in the crush stakes. Often in tense work situations it was only too easy to develop strong emotional bonds with someone, bonds which often did not hold up when the context changed. Nonetheless, she felt slightly nonplussed under his open and frank assessment.

All in all, she hadn't been very lucky with men in her life so far, which wasn't really saying much as she was only in her mid-twenties, but from time to time she felt a poignant angst that she no longer had a man to love, or to love her. Sometimes in quiet moments she felt the ticking of the internal clock.

For all she knew, Dan Blake might be married, with three or four children in tow. Somehow she didn't think so, though. There was something about the way he looked at her, a very masculine perusal of controlled interest…

'Clover,' she said, 'not Glover. I'm Signy Clover.'

'As in the flower?' he said, raising eyebrows that were dark in contrast to the straight fair hair that flopped to one side over his forehead. The hair didn't make him look boyish, as it might have done on someone else. To her he looked completely adult, very experienced, hard, not a man to be crossed, she suspected.

'Yes,' she said.

'Hey, that's cute,' he said, his very masculine mouth twisting slightly in a wry grin.

Signy thought that perhaps he was being a little sarcastic, and decided that she didn't like him. Maybe I'm being paranoid, she told herself uncertainly. These days she didn't always trust her own judgement where people were concerned. Usually she didn't prejudge people, preferring to give them many chances, to give them the benefit of the doubt at first until they either proved themselves worthy, or confirmed her thoughts. Anyway, she didn't have to like him. When this four-month retreat and training period was over she would almost certainly never see this man again.

'I'm Dan Blake,' he said, holding out a hand to her, then gripping hers firmly. 'Welcome to Canada and to British Columbia. Sorry to have kept you waiting. I'm trying to organize about half a dozen things at once. I'm going to be flying you and Ms Carpenter—when she shows up—to the island.'

'It's all right,' she said. 'It gave me a chance to look at the scenery.'

'Let's get ourselves a cup of coffee while we wait for Ms Carpenter,' he said, lifting up her two larger bags effortlessly, leaving the small carry-on bag for her.

Under a calm exterior, Signy hid a nervous excitement as she followed him the few yards to the building. She was a long way from home, she knew no one in this country and she was haunted by memories of recent work experience that hadn't been pleasant. This man she was with knew something about her past, she suspected, if he was with the organization, while she knew almost nothing about him. This imbalance left her feeling a little on edge, somehow at a disadvantage, defensive. She wasn't sure at this point what position he held.

'You haven't been with World Aid Nurses very long, have you?' he said.

'No,' she confirmed. If only he knew how green she'd been when she'd signed on with the organization in London, after she had broken up with Simon. Then she had wanted to get out of the country quickly, to have a change of scene, and had requested to go to Africa. London had become poignant with memories. They had trained her quickly and sent her out, taking her at her word. Her life had taken a complete about-face, from living cosily, obliviously, with the man she loved, going to work every day to a job she enjoyed in a teaching hospital, to a place where nothing could be taken for granted other than the fact of one's mortality. She wasn't about to tell this man, Dan Blake, how naïve she had been, how shattered by what she had witnessed there.

'So you're from England?' he said, elbowing open the door for them.

'Yes,' Signy said, following him into a utilitarian, all-purpose room. As she glanced around her quickly, she could see that it was part reception, part waiting room, freight office, and area of relaxation for staff.

'Hi, Dan. Good to see you,' several people called to him, passing through, while he raised a casual arm to them in greeting.

Perhaps this guy was the embodiment of the term 'laid back', Signy thought, grinning to herself. The observation made her wonder, and hope, that perhaps her sense of humour was finally coming back, having thought over the past six months that she had lost it for ever. Once again she pushed those nagging memories and images from the forefront of her mind, where she didn't want them to intrude during the day. It was bad enough that they plagued her nights...

'We can leave the bags here,' he said, putting them down by the door.

Signy followed him over to the corner of the room where two coffee-urns were set up on a utilitarian table, together with several trays of doughnuts and biscuits. Surreptitiously she eyed Dan Blake as he led the way, noting that he was very thin, albeit hard and muscular, as though he had, perhaps, been ill and lost weight. The light khaki-coloured trousers that he wore hung on him loosely, as did the shirt with the sleeves rolled up. As though to belie this observation, the thinness was contrasted by the tanned skin of his face and arms.

'Help yourself to coffee, Signy,' he said. 'May I call you that?'

'Yes…please,' she said, softening a little towards him, warmed by his politeness. These days most men left her indifferent, as though her experiences in Africa, her failed loves, had wrung her out emotionally, had used up all her reserves. She didn't pretend that she could understand it; for now, she was just going to go with the moment.

'And I assume I can call you Dan?' she asked.

'Sure,' he said, as he helped himself to coffee. 'When did you get in from England?'

'I came in yesterday,' she said, recalling the long flight from London, after which she had recuperated in a downtown hotel. 'I really needed that night's sleep.'

'I'm sure you did,' he said, watching her as she helped herself to coffee. With a quick flick of his wrist he looked at his watch and added, 'I trust that Ms Carpenter won't keep us waiting much longer.'

'I'm not sure exactly who you are,' Signy said apologetically. 'Are you our pilot? I was originally expecting a Dr Max Seaton…although I didn't know exactly where

I'd be meeting him. Then there was a message at the hotel to say that I would be meeting you.'

'I'm the pilot this time,' he said, his shrewd blue-grey eyes going over her features. 'I'm also one of the medical guys who will be on Kelp Island, some of the time, with your group.'

'Oh…you're Dr Blake?'

He nodded. 'Yes. You'll be meeting Max Seaton later. Maybe he's already on the island, I don't know. We should all be there by lunchtime. As I expect you know, we'll be using this weekend for rest and orientation to the surroundings.'

Signy digested this information, having taken him for something other than a medical man. Perhaps it was the broken nose, and the absence of any apparent ego that had made her jump to that conclusion. There was also something in his manner that hinted at a certain antipathy to Dr Max Seaton. Having worked for years with many different people of all types, in a wide variety of settings, she had become adept at picking up nuances and vibes from people, reading between the lines. She sensed that Dan could do the same.

'We have at least a couple of things in common,' he said. 'I have an English mother…spent some of my childhood and schooling in Devon, where we still have a home. My father's Canadian, which is why I'm in this part of the world. The other thing is that I was also in Africa.'

Something seemed to click into place with Signy. She'd had a sense that he'd been there, from the thinness, the ingrained, yellowish tan, the aura of exhaustion not quite left behind. Those were all the things that she had experienced, and a lot more besides.

'With World Aid Doctors?' she asked.

'Yes.'

'Do you work with them all the time?'

'No, just once in a while, when they need me. I'm a working doctor here. I have to earn a living, maintain commitments here.'

'I see,' she said politely, knowing that most doctors who worked with World Aid Doctors did a certain number of weeks a year in their vacation time from regular jobs, or on leave of absence, to go where they were needed around the world. Others stayed longer, those who hadn't settled on a permanent career pattern.

'Did you get involved in any wars in Somalia?' he asked.

'Not directly,' Signy said, hesitating, reluctant to talk about it now while outside the sun was shining with a pleasant, bearable heat, the ocean was very blue, the sky the same. It all felt very benign and safe, and she wanted to savour that. 'We did have some...trouble, which meant that we had to...um...get out in a hurry.' What an understatement that was, she thought with the usual pangs of regret and bitterness that came flooding back to disturb her spurious calm. 'Otherwise...it was mostly disease, malnutrition and starvation.'

Dan was aware of her reluctance as he looked at her discerningly, his eyes narrowing slightly as he took in her stiff features, as though he was aware of the effort it took her to keep her equilibrium. Then he shifted his gaze through a window that looked out over the area where he had just greeted her. 'Ah!' he said. 'It looks as though the tardy Ms Carpenter has just arrived. Excuse me.'

As Signy stood, sipping coffee, glad that they had been interrupted and watching out of the window, he strode out to meet a young woman who was just scrambling from a taxi, dropping bags as she came. The taxi driver unloaded more bags. This must be Terri Carpenter, Signy surmised as she watched a tall, slim, blonde young woman with very short spiky hair gather her bags around her then turn to shake hands with Dan. She would be one of the other nurses with the organization who would be sharing the retreat-cum-training session with her on Kelp Island.

It was a very small island off the coast of British Columbia which had once been a military base, so Signy had read in the information that had been sent to her. In fact, World Aid Nurses and World Aid Doctors were using the buildings of this now disused base, which had been built during the Second World War and added to since. Signy expected the accommodation to be somewhat spartan but comfortable, with the necessary amenities of modern living.

She finished her coffee and went outside, shifting her baggage with her, one bag at a time. As she went through the motions automatically, she was aware of her own vulnerability, of feelings that had been stirred up by this man's questions.

Dan Blake—Dr Blake—had seemed anxious to get going, so she didn't want to be the one to hold him up now. She found that she was having difficulty in thinking of him as a doctor. Not that she had a stereotyped view of what a doctor should be like, she told herself. It was just that he looked like someone who made his living out of doors. He also had that unassuming air that she found slightly disconcerting, she wasn't sure why.

In her experience so far, many doctors had at least a touch of arrogance, although World Aid Doctors tended to differ somewhat from the common mould. Perhaps some doctors were arrogant because they were making life-and-death decisions for other people, taking the initiative away from those people. Some of the best doctors she had known had acquired a degree of humility over the years, conscious that they could make and break lives, could make mistakes that could have dire consequences.

She sighed, once again pushing down images and memories that haunted her. With determination, she looked at the blue sky, the haze that hung over the water, the green mountains.

'Meet Terri Carpenter,' Dan Blake said to her when they came over.

'Great to meet you,' Terri said, extending a hand. Her pale hair, tanned skin and hazel eyes contrasted dramatically with Signy's appearance, with her paler skin, chestnut-coloured hair cut in a neat bob and blue eyes. Beside her, Signy felt a little washed out, certainly not as overtly fit and athletic.

'Signy Clover,' she said, smiling. 'Good to meet you, too.'

'I'd like to get going now, if that's all right with you,' Dan said. Then we'll be on the island in time for lunch. It will take us about twenty minutes to get there.'

'Yeah, great!' the Australian girl enthused. 'I'm ready when you are. I'll get my gear together.'

'It's just the three of us,' Dan said. 'If we can get the plane up in the air with all these bags.' He grinned wryly to belie any implied criticism in his words.

'Oh, have I got too much?' Terri asked innocently, looking around her for the first time to see what Signy had with her, then realizing that she had considerably more luggage.

'A little more than the stipulated maximum,' Dan said crisply. Signy couldn't tell whether he was really amused or annoyed.

'My excuse is that I'm a long way from home,' Terri said.

They all helped to stow the bags in the tiny plane that was waiting at the dock.

'Has either one of you been on a float plane before?' Dan asked after they had clambered inside the cabin and he had indicated the seats they should have. The aircraft would take no more than six people.

'I have,' Terri said, while Signy shook her head.

'You might want to put these on,' he said, handing them each a headset with earpieces, 'just before we take off. It can be pretty noisy. Fasten your seats belts and keep them on.'

'This looks like a great place,' Terri said to Signy as she sat down behind her. 'Maybe we'll have a chance to look around some time.'

'I hope so,' Signy agreed, taking an instant liking to the other nurse. 'I got in yesterday, so I didn't see much…just had time for a walk around downtown, near the hotel.'

'Same here. You're English, eh?'

Signy nodded.

'Are you on a retreat, as well as doing a bit more training?'

'Yes. I'm really looking forward to the retreat part of it,' Signy confirmed, smiling back.

'I am, too,' Terri said, a momentary shadow wiping the smile from her face. Signy knew from personal experience that such a remark, a casual understatement, masked the angst that came with the work they had to do, the sights they had seen.

'Were you in Africa?' Signy asked.

'East Timor.'

'Ah…' She didn't need to ask more at that moment. Immediately her mind's eye flipped the pages of a mental map and focussed on that part of the world.

Dan was in the pilot's seat, ready to go. 'Buckled up?' he said, looking over his shoulder at them. 'Put on your mufflers now.' With his own headset in place, he began a check of the controls.

Even with her hearing muffled, the roar of the engine sounded deafening to Signy. Facing front resolutely, never having liked flying very much, she clenched her hands over the armrests of her seat.

Soon they were skimming over the surface of the water, the floats sending up plumes of spray on either side. Then they were lifting up at a sharp angle, with a clear view of the mountains, the densely wooded slopes, the sparkling water of the Pacific Ocean as the sunlight struck the surface. Out there to the north was China.

Only when they had reached their desired altitude, as the land slid away and they turned south over the water, did Signy relax somewhat and release her grip. Over to her left the coast was clearly visible as they flew south. Soon they would go farther out into the ocean, over a series of small islands to Kelp Island, on the Canadian side of the border with the United States. She thought briefly of other journeys, less tranquil, that she'd made in the recent past, when she'd been in physical danger and had had to be constantly alert to what had been going on around her in case certain sights and happenings had meant danger.

To a certain extent she had thrived on it. Beyond that certain point, those moments of potential danger had put all other worries and concerns into perspective pretty quickly. That was the most positive thing that World Aid Nurses had done for her—it had all certainly been give and take, she mused now. Then she pushed the past from her mind, determined to enjoy the here and now.

Soon they were over the south end of Vancouver Island,

a very large island, well populated, off Vancouver city.
Signy remembered it from a map she had studied of the
whole area. It was mid-September, sunny and warm. The
weather would change soon, to become more unpredict-
able; it would be cooler, with quite a lot of rain, with low
cloud and mist.

Just as she was getting used to the view of the ocean
and small, densely wooded islands, the plane began to
lose height. Craning in her seat, she saw an island dead
ahead, a green, irregular spot, with no other islands immediately near it. That, she assumed, was Kelp Island.

Excitement gripped her as she anticipated the weeks
ahead in this safe, tranquil place. Up to now she hadn't
allowed herself to think too much about her need to let
go, to truly relax and recuperate—the promise of this island retreat had somehow seemed too unreal. Now, as
they were losing height, the island began to take on a
reality, and she could see forest, a shoreline.

Dan glanced briefly over his shoulder. 'We're going
down,' he shouted. 'Buckle up, if you're not already. Life
vests under seats.'

His terse remarks jerked Signy to a more immediate
reality. Looking behind her, she gave Terri a brief grin,
before checking that she did indeed have a life vest under
her seat.

The plane came down on the water quite far from the
island, then taxied noisily towards a dock. As they got
close they could see someone waiting, and two Jeep-like
utilitarian vehicles. Because this place had been a military
base there had to be at least one good road, Signy assumed, taking in as much as she could of the scene
through the tiny window. How different it was from the
dry brown of the small piece of Africa that she had
known.

She unfastened her seat belt and stood up stiffly when the craft had come to a halt at the dock. On the seat in front of her Dan had deposited a small bag of his own, plus a pile of papers, and Signy's eyes looked idly over these as she waited for the door to be opened. Something registered sharply on her consciousness, yet for a few moments she couldn't exactly place what it was. On the top sheet of a pile of papers that were secured by an elastic band, a name had been typed in quite large letters: 'R.D.H. Blake, MD'.

Something seemed to clench in her heart as she looked at that name, a sense of shock so intense that she felt momentarily faint and sick, actually felt the blood draining from her face. Quickly she sat back down in her seat, groping for her carry-on bag that she had put at her feet, taking her time about it so that she could keep her head bent down. She thought she might pass out.

That name! It hadn't occurred to her that Dan Blake might be R.D.H. Blake, the same person who had made the decision in Africa that had led directly, in her opinion, to Dominic's death. It was that person who had ordered them to leave the medical station while Dominic had still been missing out in the bush, to get out because the situation for them had become dangerous with the advent of rebels in the area where they had been working. The word 'rebel', she had discovered, was a catch-all name given to anyone who was willing to resort to violence to get what he, or his group, wanted. After a while it had become meaningless to her.

Blake was, after all, a quite common surname. Could this Dan Blake be the same Blake who had issued orders from a distance, where another World Aid group had been working, for them to get out, to leave the station and proceed immediately to a distant airstrip where they could be airlifted out? A truck had come for them with an order in writing, from him, for them to leave. No prior warning had been given in an area where communication was difficult.

As her mind took in all the possibilities, she somehow came to the conclusion that they were one and the same person.

Terri moved past her in the narrow aisle, encumbered with small bags. Dan had the door to the aircraft open. Sluggishly Signy moved forward with her own bag, her mind in overdrive.

'Are you all right? You look pale.' There he was, standing by the door, tall and very masculine in the confined space, looking at her with concern. As she came level with him he put a hand on her arm. Hypocrite! She wanted to hiss the word at him.

'Just a bit of motion sickness,' she said flatly, getting the words out with difficulty through lips that felt stiff. 'I...I'll be all right once I get out on land, get some fresh air.'

He nodded, looking beyond her out the door to the bright sunshine, still holding her arm. 'Go carefully,' he said.

Signy recoiled from him, steadying herself, pulling her arm out of his grasp. The 'D' of the middle initial of that doctor in Africa could be the 'D' for Daniel, she speculated as she moved forward. Again, that speculation hardened into certainty. Quite a lot of people she knew didn't use the first name that had been given to them in babyhood by ambitious, facetious or otherwise misguided parents, but chose instead the more acceptable alternative, or had it chosen for them by friends.

They clambered out, to be met by a youngish man wearing overalls. Signy placed her feet carefully on the wooden dock and moved forward, feeling as she had when she'd heard about Dominic's fate—sobered, intensely sad. After that first shock at the time, she'd felt long afterwards that she'd been sleep-walking, just going through the motions of being alive. Now the irony of the situation hit her...that she was here on a retreat with the very person who was in some way associated with her former mental trauma. It wasn't surprising really. World Aid Doctors, and its associated nursing branch, constituted a small group.

'Welcome to Kelp Island,' the other man said, with a Scottish accent, to her and Terri. 'I'm Jock McGregor.'

'What's a Scotsman doing here?' Signy asked, forcing herself to speech and to smile at the same time, willing herself back to the moment, as she dumped her bag on the dock and looked around appreciatively. She had to take her time to decide what she should do about Dan Blake...if anything. In spite of her shock, there was no denying the overwhelming immediacy, the austere beauty, of this place, with its dark green towering forest, and the effect it had on one. It was good to be on land again.

'Oh, we're all over the world,' he said. 'Same as the English. I'm in what you might call general maintenance.'

'I'm Terri Carpenter,' said the other young woman, the first to extend her hand.

'Hi,' he said.

'I'm Signy Clover. Nice to meet you,' she said in turn.

The first things that Signy noticed were the smells, predominantly the fresh sea air scented with the unfamiliar odour of cedar trees, and she took several deep, calming breaths. There was a moistness in the air that accentuated all the scents of nature, the soil itself, the vegetation.

'Wow!' Terri breathed the word softly. 'Just look at those trees. Some of those must be several hundred years old. I wonder why the loggers didn't get their hands on those.'

The forest rose above them on slopes, impenetrable, it seemed, apart from a narrow road that disappeared among them just beyond the dock area. All was pristine, fresh and silent, apart from the slap of water against the pilings of the dock.

Between the four of them they loaded the luggage and some other supplies into the two vehicles.

'Ride with me, Signy,' Dan said. 'Terri, you go with Jock.'

'Right,' Terri said, getting into the front of the first vehicle.

Signy opened her mouth to protest, then closed it again, a strange, passive lethargy coming over her, like a cloak of fate. Before she jumped to conclusions, she had to find out more about him. Besides, she had to work with him. Nonetheless, she felt like a trapped animal, her antipathy feeling as though it would choke her. Strange how you felt emotion in your throat, and in the region of your heart. No one really understood the physiology of that.

'Is the road OK, Jock?' Dan asked. 'Any washouts?'

'It's pretty good,' Jock said, 'apart from the inevitable potholes.'

The Scotsman, with Terri, went on ahead, disappearing slowly into the dense screen of trees. Soon there was silence again, giving Signy the opportunity to look around her at the rugged shoreline where narrow strips of sand edged the water below tumbled grey rocks. She felt uncomfortable now, alone with Dan, so much so that she thought he must sense it. Also she found herself uncommonly aware that she was a woman alone with a strange man in a very isolated spot. Irritated with herself, she forced herself to look at him as they stood together. She considered the slightly twisted nose, the thin, oddly attractive, exhausted face.

'What do you think of the island so far?' he said.

Signy swallowed. 'It's...it's beautiful,' she said, meaning it. 'But...not benign, I think.'

At that he smiled slightly, looking at her perceptively. 'Mmm,' he agreed.

'I assume the smell is the scent of cedar trees?' she said.

'Yes. On some other parts of the island there are some sandy beaches. Very wild, some of them, facing the ocean, with spectacular breakers. A lot of kelp gets washed up there. Hence the name.'

'I hope we'll get time to explore some of them,' she said, picturing the wild, deserted beaches.

'You will,' he said. 'I'll show you some time, if you like.'

Immediately Signy was wary, withdrawing into herself, as she had done over the past weeks since she had come back from Africa.

'Thank you,' she said stiffly, knowing that her recoil had been obvious.

'It's part of the treatment,' he said, a brusque note in his voice. 'Lots of walks in the mist and rain, through the forest trails, on blustery beaches. Let the exertion of the body heal the mind.'

Signy's cheeks slowly suffused with colour. He had immediately tuned in to her standoffishness and censure, and she felt a sharp regret. It wasn't her custom to judge before she had all the facts, so she told herself to hold off. Her excuse was that she was still in love with Simon...or was it Dominic, whom she had met for the first time in Africa? Perhaps it hadn't been love, but certainly she had formed a very strong bond with him and still mourned him acutely. She needed some time to be alone now on her walks, to think, to sort things out in her mind, so she told herself.

'I didn't mean...' she began hesitantly.

'No, neither did I,' he said. 'Let's go. Do you have some sort of jacket you can put on? It can get quite cool in the woods.'

'Yes.' Glad of the diversion, she fumbled in her carry-on bag to pull out a knitted jacket. She had a lightweight rain jacket in there too, against the frequent falls of rain that were typical in the area.

In the forest much of the sunlight was shut out, putting them into a dim green light that seemed to Signy mysterious and unworldly, so that she shivered and pulled the jacket closely around her. Dan drove slowly and carefully. The scents of trees, ferns, moss and moist soil came in through the windows. The paved road, more of a lane, was narrow and uneven, bordered on either side by clumps of ferns, trees and other vegetation that she didn't recognize. Sitting there beside this man, whom she was convinced had affected her life in the recent past, even though they had never met, it made her feel that, rather than getting away from the past, it was coming back to greet her, to encompass her once more.

'You have a background in operating theatre work and emergency nursing, Signy, so I remember from my brief perusal of your CV,' Dan said, breaking the slightly strained silence that had sprung up between them. Signy wondered whether it was all on her side. So far he had given no indication that her name meant anything to him. If it had, he wouldn't have called her 'Glover'.

He turned to look at her for a moment, his glance shrewd and appraising, before he turned back to view the road which had suddenly deteriorated slightly. They slowed down to go around some potholes, the vehicle climbing steadily away from the dock. 'And you've done some midwifery training?' he added.

'Yes,' she confirmed.

'I'm surprised you got sent out to Africa,' he said, 'as your first assignment. That was rather throwing you in at the deep end.' To her heightened awareness, his comment sounded like a criticism of her, perhaps implying that she couldn't have been expected to cope.

'I wanted to go there,' she said tightly. 'I could have refused, I had the option. At the time the place I was sent to was not considered particularly dangerous. At least, not any more dangerous than any other place. As you know, situations can change quickly, and unforeseen things happen. You don't always have time to get out when perhaps you should.'

'No…you're quite right,' he murmured, telling her nothing.

With tension rising in her beyond endurance, Signy decided to test him. 'Some of my party were taken hostage by a rebel group. Fortunately they got away eventually, but for a while no one knew what the outcome would be… We expected the worst.' At that moment she didn't want to tell him that Dr Dominic Fraser, one of her three abducted colleagues, hadn't come back to the medical station when he should have done, had decided—with misguided bravado, it seemed now—to link up with members of the UN forces in an attempt to track down his captors. He hadn't made it back in time to be driven out when the others had been evacuated.

'That's pretty grim, and it happens quite commonly,' Dan said. 'The best thing is to get out when there's the first hint of possible trouble. There's no point in becoming

a liability or a casualty yourself. I wouldn't have thought
you were the right person for that setting.'

'Oh? Why not?' she said.

'Don't take this wrong. You seem very…what shall I
say? Fragile.'

Signy searched around for words, not knowing what to
say. 'Appearances can be deceptive,' she said. The only
way she was fragile at the moment, she found herself
thinking, was emotionally, and she didn't think he was
referring to that.

'What exactly is your role here on the island?' she said,
thinking it was time to shift attention away from herself,
knowing that she sounded at least mildly belligerent. Determined not to show that his words had hurt her, after all
she had been through, she stared blankly ahead. Obviously
the scene in Africa, one of many for him, she suspected,
hadn't rung any particular bells in his memory, while for
her it dominated her life. 'Are you involved in the training
course?'

'Yes. I also work in some of the small community hos-
pitals and clinics in some of the outlying areas, partly on
a consultant basis, partly routine,' he said matter-of-factly.
'It's a hectic life. I sometimes take you, the nurses, with
me. Mainly my role is to show you what it's like to work
in small communities that are isolated, or more or less so.
The information you pick up is of help when you go on
assignments. You learn to plan ahead in great detail, to
rely on your own devices.'

'I did learn that in Africa,' she pointed out.

He gave her a quick glance and said nothing, while she
chalked up one point to herself. He was being a bit overbearing.

'Are you a surgeon?' she said.

'I have done surgery,' he said, 'mainly trauma. Then I

trained in obstetrics. I find myself doing a bit of everything, whatever's needed. It became very obvious on my
assignments abroad, in emergency and disaster situations,
that there was a great need for someone to take care of
pregnant women.'

Signy nodded, somewhat surprised, not having taken
him for an obstetrician. Really, she didn't know what to
make of him. One minute Dan seemed overbearing, then
the next he gave out glimpses of something else, a surprising sensitivity. Anyway, she made up her mind to be
wary of him.

'Can you fly a plane or drive a motorboat?' he asked,
peering ahead where the headlights of the car cast a yellow glow on the green gloom. Here and there shafts of
sunlight slanted through tall trees, some of which appeared to be very old, tall and massive, with moss clinging
to their trunks.

'No,' she said, beginning to feel a little alarmed again
that this man might find her wanting in his estimation,
perhaps useless in the training that lay ahead. She knew
that fear was part of her problem, part of her need to rest,
to be in a tranquil place. One doctor had told her that she
was suffering from survivor's guilt. 'Do I need to?'

'Not specifically. What can you do? Apart from your
work, that is.' He asked with what seemed to her subtle
sarcasm.

'I can swim,' she said, 'row or sail a small boat, drive
a car, truck or tractor, ride a horse. I have ridden a motorbike.' If only he knew about that last bit, she thought
succinctly, some of her old confidence coming back. Well,
she would save that for some other time, for when she
needed to assert herself. That image of herself riding
through scrubland on a motorbike with an injured man on
the back, who clung to her like a dead weight, never left

her. Yes, she would clobber Dan Blake with that when the need arose.

He turned to look at her, his eyebrows raised. 'Can you ski?' he said.

'I have been skiing,' she said carefully, 'but I wouldn't really say that I can ski. It seemed a pointless exercise at the time.'

'Mmm.'

It appeared to Signy again, sensitive to criticism, that there was a wealth of meaning in that usually noncommittal sound—a meaning that was negative.

'There were no planes or motorboats where I was in Somalia,' she said tartly. 'It was subsistence living...if you could call it living. Mostly it was starvation. And there was no snow.' She added the last bit emphatically.

The words were out before she could help herself, because his questioning irritated her when she felt herself to be a seasoned person in the field. At the same time she knew that this man would be in a position to judge her throughout the training course. He would be one of the people to make pronouncements at the end. 'I would have done almost anything for a bit of snow,' she said.

He turned to her and laughed. 'Point taken,' he said.

Signy felt disarmed by his grin, also contrarily annoyed, conscious that she had been holding herself stiffly away from him, careful not to let her arm brush against his as the vehicle swayed and bounced over some of the rougher parts of the road. The amusement on his face made him look so much younger, attractive...

She looked away. 'One thing I can do, Dr Blake,' she said, 'is take care of myself. I can also see a job through. I've done a lot. Now I'm mainly here because I need a rest.'

'Yes,' he said softly, agreeing. 'I didn't mean to goad you, Signy.'

'Funny,' she said, not particularly caring what he thought of her at that moment, 'I could have sworn you did.'

'Just want to know what you're all about. There isn't much time.'

'All right,' she said. 'So long as it's a two-way street. Some people like to ask a lot of personal questions, but they're not so good at disclosing personal information about themselves. That always strikes me as being a bit flaky, as though knowing all the answers puts them in a one-up position. Are you one of those, Dr Blake?'

'I like to think not,' he said quietly. 'I do need to know something about you…and if there's anything you want to know about me, just ask away.'

'All right,' she said. 'Well, to let you know more about me…let me see…I can respond to a crisis appropriately, I can hold together. In fact, I think I work better that way, which is probably why I like operating theatre and emergency work. People are different in a crisis.' She was forcing herself to be polite, feeling as though she was making small-talk, when her sense of shock at seeing his name was still dominating her emotions.

'Right,' he said. 'They show their true selves.'

They went on for a while in silence.

'And how did you break your nose?' she asked, out of the blue, since he was being very inquisitive. 'I think I could picture you in a fight.' That much was true. There was a hardness about him that contrasted with the suspected sensitivity, which made her sure that he would be able to make a decision quickly in a crisis and stick to it. Hadn't he done that with Dominic?

Again he smiled. 'Fell out of a tree,' he said.

'That mundane!' Signy was disarmed.

'Mmm. When I was sixteen. We were out in some remote place, a small group of us, hiking out here, when I was on holiday from England.'

'And you never got it fixed?' Signy said, looking sideways at his enigmatic profile. The Jeep bounced and swayed over more potholes.

'There happened to be a doctor on hand to give me first aid,' he said. 'It hurt like hell, I was bleeding all over the place and I fainted. When we got back to civilization I didn't bother to get further treatment, even though my mother was horrified and said it would ruin my beauty.' Dan grinned. 'I was too much of a coward.'

An odd sort of truce, if one could call it that when there wasn't really a declared war, had occurred between them. It was a delicate balance. For purposes of his own he had been sounding her out. So far, she wasn't ready to talk about details or divulge that she'd recognized his name.

They drove on without speaking for quite a while, the road taking them farther into the central part of the island. Beyond the military camp the road would continue to the other side of the island where there were some of the sandy beaches that he had mentioned earlier.

'The camp is quite civilized,' Dan said. 'The barracks have been divided up into individual rooms. There are plenty of communal areas as well, even a bar.'

'Sounds all right,' she said.

At last they were there, coming out suddenly from the shade of the trees into a very large, cleared site, with narrow roads and paths crisscrossing between several single-storey buildings. From what Signy could see, it all looked very well tended and not too spartan at all.

'There are no trees in the camp,' Signy observed.

'That's right. It's to guard against the effects of forest

fires, so they can't spread into the camp via trees, one hopes. Once in a while a tree is struck by lightning, and that can start a fire if everything's dry, although here we usually get a fair amount of rain in the summer. Also, one less thing to fall on top of a building, or person, if there's an earthquake.'

'Earthquake?' Signy said, looking at him in alarm. 'Are you joking?'

'No,' he said lightly. 'They seldom happen, but this is an earthquake zone. Don't worry about it.'

Just as Signy was wondering how he could come out with something like that, then tell her not to worry about it, he brought the Jeep to a halt outside a small wooden building with a shingled roof, so she swallowed the questions that she wanted to ask. A sign stated RECEPTION: ALL VISITORS MUST REPORT HERE.

'We'll find out where your room is,' Dan said. 'That's the mess building over there. That's where they serve lunch.' He indicated a building in the centre of the base.

Inside Reception they were greeted by a young woman with short hair, wearing military-style khaki shorts with many pockets, a shirt of the same colour with tabs on the shoulders and rolled-up sleeves. A sign on the desk indicated that she was called Sabrina.

'Hi, Dan,' she said.

'Hi, Sabrina,' he said.

'Hi,' she said to Signy. 'What name?'

'Signy Clover.'

'Clover…' She ran her finger down a list. 'You're in Moose Head.'

'Um…' Signy said uncertainly. Beside her she could feel rather than see Dan's amusement.

'That's the name of the hut you're in,' he said lightly.

'Don't be put off by the name, it's a comfortable place. Come on, I'll help you with the bags.'

Outside Reception there were some luggage trolleys, one of which Dan grabbed to load their bags onto. 'I'm over that way,' he pointed. 'I have a little hut to myself called Holly Berry. Feel free to call on me if you need anything.'

'Is Sabrina one of us? I mean, one of the World Aid nurses?'

'No, she works in the camp,' he said. 'Her domain is Kelp Island. There are twelve nurses—if they've all shown up. I've flown some of them here.'

The door was open to Moose Head, a long, squat building that had clearly been a barracks, and Terri was at the door. 'Hello,' she greeted them. 'This place is absolutely wonderful. Not what I imagined at all. We're in the same building.'

'That's great,' Signy said, pleased, and they lugged her bags to her room. When Dan left she felt oddly relieved, so much so that she let out a sigh.

The room was painted in a pale yellow, with dark pink woodwork around the window, the door and the baseboards, making the whole place look charming, so that Signy found herself smiling. There were bright coloured curtains and a thick duvet with a cover in the same pattern on the bed, over blankets. The room was fully furnished, in a simple style, with all the basics that she could possibly need.

'This is lovely,' she said, looking round her. 'Not quite what I expected.'

'Hello!' a masculine voice called from the main doorway, bringing them both out of Signy's room.

The man who stood inside the threshold—in a small sitting-room area, which had a kitchenette off it—was tall, muscular, dark-haired, blue-eyed and very handsome. Terri and Signy stood looking at him silently. Even though he was casually dressed, he looked somehow out of place. There was a certain elegance and sophistication about him that didn't seem to go well with a hut named Moose Head and the picture of a cartoon moose that someone had tacked to the inside wall just above the door.

'Hi,' he said. 'I just wanted to meet you, to introduce myself.' He held out a hand. 'I'm Max Seaton. The plan is that we'll all meet for lunch in the mess at twelve-thirty, then afterwards I want to talk to you all about what to expect from the programme here.'

When he took Signy's hand and held onto it a fraction longer than was strictly appropriate for a simple hand-shake, she uncharacteristically found herself melting, her mouth stretching into a warm smile. 'How do you do?' she said, the first thing that came into her head.

'Ms Clover,' he said, 'I'm very much looking forward to getting to know you. And you, Ms Carpenter.' When he turned his charm on Terri, holding out his hand, she stood with her mouth slightly open, looking at him. 'See you in a short while.'

'Now, *he*,' Terri said, gazing after him from the open door as he strode away, 'isn't quite what *I* expected!'

CHAPTER TWO

LUNCH in the mess hut was a casual self-service affair, and the food was good. Each nurse wore a name tag, while Sabrina was there to make sure that they were introduced to one another.

The twelve nurses were of varying ages, some appearing to be in their twenties, some in their thirties, while two were older than the others, perhaps early forties, Signy guessed. It was good to see such an age spread, with obviously a great deal of experience among them all. One of the older women was named Connie, and Signy found herself sitting between her and Terri at a long refectory-type table. Dan and Max Seaton were also there. Signy couldn't help noticing that Terri's eyes strayed to Dr Seaton very frequently, as did those of some of the other women. In some ways he seemed out of context, more suited to a film set, perhaps, in front of the cameras.

After the meal Dr Seaton rose to his feet and went to the head of the room where there was a slightly raised platform and a makeshift lectern.

'I think I've met you all,' he said with a smile, his voice a low drawl. 'In case there are one or two I've missed, I'm Max Seaton. For some of the time I will be here on the island to talk to you about medicine under difficult circumstances, medicine in remote and semi-remote places. Dr Dan Blake will also be working in that capacity, among other things. Between the two of us, we shall invite you to observe us at work.' He paused to smile around at his rapt, silent audience. Signy found herself staring with the rest.

'You've all been asked to obtain registration in this province. That is so you have the right to enter a hospital, accompanied by one of us, to observe procedures there, and so that you can go to outlying places to help the doctors and nurses. You will find that it is the nurses who service many of these places, who deliver many of the babies, make diagnoses. I for one never under-estimate the value of nurses, or under-appreciate the work they do. Where a doctor may be a rarity, there is a nursing station to serve a remote community. Assignments will be given to you, which you will find posted on the noticeboard here in the mess.'

When Max had finished speaking, Dan got up.

'The remainder of this weekend,' he said, his unassuming manner contrasting with the charm of the previous man, 'will be given over to rest, relaxation and orientation to this camp and to the island in general. Some of you have come a very long way, so we appreciate that you need to sleep. Get to know one another. In the future with the organization, some of you may well be working together. This is a retreat, as well as a training base. One of my jobs is to give counselling if it's needed. You have only to ask. Nothing is forced upon you.'

Signy wondered whether she could unburden herself to this man about her work in Africa…about Simon, about Dominic…and she smiled wryly to herself, trying to imagine his reaction if she wanted to talk about the men she had loved.

'For the next two weeks,' he was saying, 'you will remain on the island, have lectures and informal talks and get orientated. You will also learn how to find your way around in places like this.'

Signy was listening, yet part of her mind was detached. What would this man's reaction be when—or if—she confronted him about her time in Africa and his order that had evacuated their medical station and left Dominic unaccounted for? Her mind wandered as she stared unseeingly into space, concentrating on the past. Would she find the courage to confront him?

Dan went on talking for some time, then he said, 'One thing I must ask, for your safety, is that if you go for a walk from the camp, please, sign out in the logbook that is on the desk in Reception, stating the time you leave the camp, the precise details of where you are going and the expected time of your return to the camp.' He paused, his eyes roving over the small assembled group of nurses. Unlike Max, he didn't smile. There was something about his manner that underscored the seriousness of what he was saying.

'This is so that we can look for you if, for some reason, you are late getting back. There are maps at the desk so, please, take one with you at all times. It's easy to get lost on the trails through the forest, especially at dusk, even though each trail is named and signposted. Although this is a relatively small island, it is densely forested, and all trails tend to look the same, especially at dusk,' he went on. 'Don't deviate from the route you've stated you'll be on. Fortunately, there are no grizzly or black bears on this island, no cougars or coyotes, no wolves. There are bears in other areas of this province, as there are all those other animals that I mentioned, although not all together, generally, in the same place. How to deal with wild animals will be covered in a separate talk at a later date by an expert on bears. Bears can and do kill humans.'

There was a rapport in the room. At least half the nurses present had been on work assignments to places where there were crises, that weren't safe for workers. As they listened they were, Signy suspected, thinking back to those places, as she was herself. There was sometimes a very thin line between being safe and not being safe, between life and death. And the reality of having survived, having been on the right side of that very fine line, left its own trauma. There was an empathy and camaraderie in their small group of professional women; Signy could feel it, because it was there in her, together with a strange kind of gratitude and humility for having survived.

Dan's eyes went over them again, pausing to make eye contact with each woman as he spoke. 'The weather can change dramatically and suddenly. Darkness can come down quickly with that change, as can mist and fog. There is a lot of persistent, heavy rain. That's why you've been asked to bring a powerful flashlight with you, a whistle and an alarm, plus a cellphone—that will work in most places here, but you still have to know where you are. Always carry them with you when you leave the camp, and wear appropriate clothing and footwear at all times for cold and rain. Although you may walk here for pleasure and to get yourselves orientated, that is also part of your basic training. Be aware of what's going on around you at all times. There will be times when you are in places less safe, when the rules of safe conduct may save your life and the lives of your colleagues.'

When he paused, the silence in the room was complete. 'Make rules for your own safety, based on your own common sense and experience, your gut feelings about a given situation and the rules that have been laid down for you by others in the field,' he said.

Signy swallowed, thinking back to her time in Somalia. She had not always followed that advice…

'Never break your own rules for safety,' Dan went on.

'That one time when you break those rules may be your last, and that applies anywhere in the world that you may live, not just in the field work that we do. It applies to even the most seemingly benign place. Very often the most dangerous predators in a place are the human ones. In any given place, at any given time, a certain percentage of the population are psychopaths, just waiting for the opportunity to do their thing.'

Again Signy swallowed a nervous lump in her throat. At the medical station in Somalia she'd refused to leave when the evacuation truck had arrived unexpectedly to take them out. She'd stated that she wouldn't leave without Dominic. Had he been foolish to go? Naïve? It was easy to judge now. She refused to think of him that way when she knew him to be a courageous, intelligent man, very good at his job and dedicated to the work of World Aid Doctors.

Again Dan looked around the small group, making eye contact with each one of them. Signy was aware that she had a self-conscious flush on her face, that the pupils of her eyes had grown large with a certain apprehension that perhaps he could somehow divine her thoughts, or perhaps knew more about her than she suspected.

'As far as you possibly can,' he said succinctly, articulating each word carefully for emphasis, 'never give them that opportunity.'

A creeping respect for this man was reluctantly imposing itself on her awareness.

'Never take short cuts, never cut corners,' Dan was saying. 'Sometimes you have seconds only in which to decide on a course of action. Always plan ahead so that you can, as far as possible, be ready.'

While Signy felt that he might be speaking just to her,

she knew that each nurse in the room had reason to feel the same.

'When dealing with people in unfamiliar cultures especially, as well as in those you are familiar with, learn the difference between trust and naïvety,' he went on. 'There is a difference. It is one thing to feel you can trust someone, another thing to behave naïvely with that person. Again, that one act of naïvety—not appropriate to an adult—could be your last. We will, of course, be talking about safety in great detail, in many types of situations, throughout this course. What I'm saying now is by way of an introduction. Any questions so far?'

Signy stood up, declining to put up her hand like a child at school. 'What about earthquakes here?' she challenged him, having had the idea that he hadn't wanted to dwell on that earlier. There was a surprised turning of heads from some of the other nurses, so at least some of them hadn't known about the possibility.

'This whole area is an earthquake zone,' he said slowly, fixing her with an enigmatic stare, 'the same as parts of California. So we have to have an idea of what to do in the event of an earthquake. That will be something we shall talk about over the next weeks. However, the likelihood is rather remote. Anything else?'

A few other people asked questions, then coffee was served, and the meeting turned into more of a social event in which people exchanged stories of their work experiences.

Signy felt a touch on her arm as she was talking to Connie.

'Excuse me. You're Signy Clover, if I remember correctly?' Max Seaton stood there, looking down at her from his superior height, while she found herself looking up into a pair of the bluest eyes she had ever seen.

'Um…yes,' she said.

'Call me Max,' he said.

Connie excused herself, leaving Signy feeling a disturbing dissonance that Dr Seaton hadn't included the other woman in his greeting. Yet he had a charm that seemed to excuse such minor infractions of what Signy termed manners. She reminded herself that she was in a different culture, that she was the one who had to adapt, so that she glanced at the other woman with a mute apology. Connie smiled slightly and moved away.

'I never pass up an opportunity to talk to an English woman,' he said. 'I spent some time in London and in Oxford.'

'I know London well, because I lived and worked there…did my nursing training there,' she said, feeling herself melting emotionally under his concentrated interest, in spite of her underlying resistance and her sharp awareness of his apparent lack of sensitivity. 'Although I grew up in Kent.'

'Tell me where you've worked there,' he asked, making her feel as though he really wanted to know, concentrating his whole attention on her. It was nice, she had to admit, to have such attention. 'Tell me all about London, what it's like now.'

'That will be easy,' she said. 'It's a city I love. I never get tired of it.'

The minutes went by while they talked, until Signy noticed that the others were leaving the room and the two of them were among the few left. Others were looking at her as they left.

'I've rather monopolized you, Dr Seaton,' she apologized, whereas it had been the other way round really.

As she looked around her she saw Dan leaving. For a moment their eyes met, and she detected a veiled question

in his regard. Perhaps he thought she was flirting with his
very attractive colleague, but nothing was further from her
mind, although it *was* nice to be in a semi-social setting
for a short while with an attractive man, no strings attached. Perhaps getting involved with someone on this
course was a no-no, although one wouldn't think it from
Dr Seaton's relaxed attitude, she thought.

'Call me Max…please,' he murmured to her. 'No, I
was monopolizing you. The pleasure has been all mine.'

'Well,' she said, 'I'd better go and do a little more
exploring of the camp so that I won't get lost if I have to
go somewhere, especially if all that mist or fog comes
down that Dr Blake was talking about.'

'He likes to scare you a bit…' Max smiled '…so that
you take notice.'

'Well, he wasn't so forthcoming about earthquakes,'
she ventured.

'Oh, the chances of that are fairly remote, so we don't
want to dwell on it more than is necessary. There are a
lot of little quakes, but they are so small that we don't
actually feel them. Quakes that are below three on the
Richter scale. They happen out at sea, most of them, and
are just picked up by seismologists at monitoring stations.'

'I see,' Signy said, not finding his words particularly
reassuring, although she suspected that if she'd heard the
same information in her past, before she had started work
with World Aid Nurses, she would have been more or
less blithely unconcerned. There was something about
having been in danger that made you more aware of it
everywhere. Or perhaps it was just that she had grown up
a bit.

'Hey, Signy!' Terri was by her side, flashing a brilliant
smile at Max. 'I was wondering if you would like to join

me on a little exploratory walk of the camp. With all the sitting on planes that I've been doing, I could use a bit of time putting one foot in front of the other.'

'Yes, I'd like that,' Signy said, feeling relieved that she could extricate herself from the slightly predatory Max.

She and Terri walked briskly away from the mess hall. 'I bet he generally gets what he wants where women are concerned,' Terri said, a cynical note in her voice, and they both laughed.

Back in the pleasant yellow and pink room in Moose Head hut, Signy went through her luggage to get out a pair of loose cotton trousers, a T-shirt and light sweater, to change out of the blouse and skirt that she was wearing. From another holdall she took out lightweight hiking boots and socks. Quickly she took a shower in the tiny *en suite* bathroom, then dressed again. She found herself wondering what Dan was doing. There was a certain relief to be away from what she felt was his supervision.

There was a knock on her door. 'May I come in?' It was Terri.

Signy let her in. 'Almost ready,' she said, towelling her hair vigorously. 'I just had to have a shower—couldn't wait.'

'Same here.' Terri smiled. 'You know, I'm really glad we met at that air terminus in Vancouver, Signy. I was rather apprehensive about coming here. I thought maybe I wouldn't have a lot in common with other people here. I've only been on one assignment abroad, and I thought maybe most of the others would be really seasoned people, maybe a bit hard-bitten.'

'I've only been on one assignment, too,' Signy said. 'Although it was so horrendous that I feel as though I've been on half a dozen. From talking to some of the other nurses, I think they're a rather humble lot, even though they've done some pretty brave things, I suspect, sort of going where angels fear to tread.'

'Yeah,' Terri said thoughtfully. 'Maybe it's more of a case of where angels tread. We're really in the minority, you know. Not very many people would go where we're prepared to go, I came to learn that. Perhaps we are what that guy Dan Blake said...naïve. I thought it was ironic really, that he was saying we need to know the difference between trust and naïvety.'

'It's a calculated risk, Terri,' Signy said, knowing that she was going to have a good rapport with this nurse. 'That's what we're doing. We have a good training and we have our common sense. The rest is up to fate. That's basically what life is all about, I suppose.'

Together they left the hut, heading for the path that went around the periphery of the camp. As they passed the reception building they saw Max again, talking to one of the other nurses.

'He's rather gorgeous, isn't he?' Terri said in a muted voice, before they were within earshot of the doctor. 'Makes you wonder what someone like him is doing here, or in the medical profession, come to that. He ought to be in films.'

'Good looks don't necessarily get you where you want to go, although maybe they give you a head start.' Signy laughed.

'You mean like the old saying, "Looks don't last, cooking do"?'

'I thought it was, "Kissing don't last, cooking do",' Signy said. They laughed together as they went past Max. He turned and looked at Signy with a quick, appraising glance from head to foot and back again.

Most of the time these days it came as a surprise to Signy when a man found her attractive, or appeared to do so. She had got used to taking that interest with the proverbial pinch of salt. That was what breaking up with Simon had done for her—it had battered her first flush of youthful confidence and self-esteem.

'I wonder what assignments Dr Seaton has been on with World Aid Doctors,' Terri murmured, her tone implying that perhaps he hadn't been on too many that could have been called remotely dangerous.

As they walked under the shade of tall, cool trees, breathing in fresh, unpolluted air, Signy recalled the offer that Dan had made to show her the beaches, and how quick she had been to rebuff him. Now she felt an odd regret, in spite of her shock and antipathy when she thought of him and what he had done, perhaps inadvertently. There was a brooding quality about him that seemed to go with the dark wildness of this place. Strange that she should be thinking that way…

At that moment she felt close to both Simon and Dominic, as though she could meet them at any moment, which was odd, as though her past and her present were coming together.

'This is great…absolutely great,' Terri breathed, looking up at the trees that towered above them. 'I'll feel safe here, I can tell.'

When they were back again at Moose Head hut and Signy was in the sanctuary of her delightful small room, she found herself pleasantly tired and relaxed by the exertion of the hike. The remainder of the day was her own until suppertime in the mess. They could also make tea in the kitchenette off the sitting room in the hut.

She took off her outer clothing and got into bed under the duvet. The temperature was pleasantly cool now, a good time to sleep. She lay there with her arms behind her head, looking up at the ceiling. How strange it was that she was in this remote place, on the edge of an ocean, with others who had the same purpose. There was a slight feeling of dissonance, yet at the same time a feeling of sanctuary. She was safe here…

Here were new people again, among whom there was the possibility that she would make some lifetime friends. With eyes closed, she thought of other situations in which she had encountered new people who had mattered… There had been Simon, never far from her thoughts—Dr Simon Heathcote, a young surgeon who had come to work in the London teaching hospital where she had been a staff nurse in the operating theatres. One day he hadn't been in her life, she hadn't known he existed, then the next morning there he'd been, and everything had changed for ever.

'Hello, you must be Signy Clover,' a masculine voice had said early on a Monday morning when she'd been intent on opening packs for the first case in her operating theatre where she'd been assigned to work for the day. 'Sister Granger told me that you would tell me where things are. I have to scrub to assist for the first case.'

She had turned round from her task, feeling under stress because time had been tight, with only minutes to get ready for the case, already feeling irritable with the owner of the voice. Then from the moment she'd encountered the blue-eyed, blond good looks of Simon Heathcote as he'd looked round the edge of the door, she'd been smitten, had known by some sort of precognition that they were to mean something to each other.

'Oh…' she'd said, pointing. 'First, get yourself a cap and mask through there, by the scrub sinks.'

They had worked together regularly from that day on. Even so, it had seemed like a fairy-tale to her that they'd been mutually attracted, had fallen in love, then a few months later had decided to live together.

Signy stirred restlessly now, turning on her side and pulling the duvet up around her ears. There was no sound discernible to her from the rest of the camp, all was peaceful. How wonderful it had been to live with Simon, to make a cosy home for them in a tiny, rather scruffy flat above a grocer's shop in the East End of London. The area had started to become trendy, but not so much so that they hadn't been able to afford to live there. They had cleaned the place up very thoroughly, had painted the walls and woodwork, working on weekends and evenings, whenever they'd had time off. She had bought pretty fabric to make curtains cheaply to make the place feel and look like a home. It had all seemed so permanent.

Nine months later Simon had told her that he was in love with someone else, a doctor with whom he'd been working over the past four weeks. Both she and Simon had been working long hours. He had been on call a lot so that when they'd started to spend less and less time together she had put it down to pressure of work.

She stayed on alone in the flat for a while, her self-esteem at its lowest point ever, then found working in the same hospital impossible, seeing Simon and his new woman every day. You didn't stop loving someone because they no longer wanted to be with you. On the contrary, in some perverse way you dwelt obsessively on their image, idealized them, longed for them every minute of the day, as well as in those moments during the night when you woke up in a panic because they were no longer there.

Looking back, she saw that she'd been complacent at first, had taken to the cosy domesticity like the proverbial duck to water, without a certain necessary cynicism, or maybe realism. She wouldn't make that mistake again. Then she read an advertisement in a nursing journal for World Aid Nurses...

Don't think about it now, she told herself. Put it out of your mind, it's all water under the bridge. Go to sleep...go to sleep.

As she drifted into sleep, the face before her inner vision wasn't that of Simon Heathcote, but the darker features of Max Seaton...and finally the angular, clean-cut features and characteristic nose of Dan Blake. No, that was R.D.H. Blake, she reminded herself. She tried to picture him as a sixteen-year-old, as his words came back to her—'fell out of a tree'. Those words had disarmed her at the time, yet now she couldn't picture him as a teenager, frightened to have surgery on his nose. He seemed completely adult. That in itself was something rare. If he was as responsible as he seemed, he wouldn't shirk from answering her questions about Africa...

It was Connie Lenz, the nurse in her forties, who knocked on Signy's door half an hour before suppertime. 'Hello, Signy,' she said with a welcoming yet tentative smile. 'The others here are having a glass of white wine before supper. Would you like to join us? It's in the kitchen.'

'Love to,' Signy said, blinking the sleep out of her eyes. 'Give me a few seconds to wake up and get dressed.'

Connie was a Canadian of mixed ancestry, so she'd explained earlier. The fourth occupant of the Moose Head hut was a West Indian nurse named Pearl James. What an interesting mixture they were. Signy smiled to herself as she dressed in a clean skirt and blouse, and eased her feet into slip-on shoes. It took her seconds only to brush her hair and put on a dash of make-up.

'Whose idea was this?' she said, as she accepted a glass

of cold white wine out in the small kitchen, where the others were standing about talking and sipping.

'Connie brought the wine,' Terri said. 'One of several.' They all laughed together.

'To us,' said Pearl, raising her glass. 'May we regain our sanity in this place, and the courage to go on, to do what we have to do.' Pearl was colourfully dressed in a flowing pink, orange and purple caftan, with a light wool shawl around her shoulders in a pale grey.

'I'll say amen to that,' Connie said. She had a tired, rather leathery face that had seen too much sun but had an expression of kindliness, humour and intelligence. 'To us!'

'To us!' they all chorused.

Signy wondered whether similar scenes were going on in the other huts. She hoped so as she sipped the very good wine. 'I needed this,' she said. 'Thank you, Connie. Are you from this part of the country?'

'Not originally,' Connie said, 'although I've worked and lived here for a while. I've worked with both Dan Blake and Max Seaton before.'

Terri perked up. 'Tell us about Max,' she said. 'Is he for real? I mean, has he got a personality to match his gorgeous exterior?'

Connie hesitated. 'I prefer not to say too much before you've had a chance to make up your own mind, more or less,' she said. 'Let me just say that men like Max ultimately disappoint because you tend to expect too much of them, and they can't oblige.'

'That's a great way of putting it,' Terri said. 'Elaborate.'

'Well…they go for what they want, without giving much thought to what the other person might want,' Connie said.

'Has he been on any long assignments?' Signy asked.

'I think he goes mainly to short-term disaster zones, hurricanes, tornadoes, floods, earthquakes, volcanic eruptions…that sort of thing,' Connie said. 'Where you do your bit and then get out.'

'What about Dan?' Signy found herself saying. 'I'm curious about him.'

'He's a different sort of person,' Connie said. 'A great doctor. I think he's really dedicated to his work, so he makes a difference wherever he goes. There was some sadness in his life, so I heard. He was living with a woman, another doctor. They'd been together for several years, so I believe, then she got fed up with him going off around the world. Apparently, she didn't mind at first, then I guess the novelty wore off and she wanted to settle down, get married, have babies. I think she gave him an ultimatum, so I heard…his work or her.'

'And he chose the work?' Pearl said.

'Yes.'

'What else is new?' Pearl said with a laugh. 'I can see where this sort of work could be addictive. You get to use every bit of skill you have.'

'Aren't we a lot of gossips?' Terri said lightly, not seeming to care. 'Where is the woman now? Married to someone else, with three or four kids?'

'As a matter of fact,' Connie said, 'she works in Vancouver as a GP, I think, and used to spend some time in the small place up the coast, Brookes Landing, where we'll be going for some of the time, so I heard. Maybe she still does. And, no, I don't think she's married.'

'Maybe she regrets giving him the ultimatum,' Pearl suggested.

'Maybe,' Connie said thoughtfully, 'but imagine how you would feel if your man, or your husband, was going off to dangerous places maybe twice a year and staying away for several weeks.'

'Mmm,' Terri murmured. 'Not exactly conducive to a harmonious married life. I've more or less decided that the moment I get serious about anyone, I won't be doing this any more…unless maybe he can come with me. What about you, Signy?'

'Well…' Signy began hesitantly, 'I guess I got into this because I was running away. At least, I wanted to get away. I haven't really thought about what I would do…' That was the nearest she had come to telling anyone about Simon, other than her parents, and she hadn't told them a great deal. Perhaps there was going to be a lot about this place that was conducive to confidences.

A bell rang, telling them it was time for supper, interrupting the details. Signy was secretly pleased that now she knew something else about Dan, after he had quizzed her; it helped her to try to put things into perspective. She could somehow picture him turning down a woman for his work. Well, it was nothing to do with her, except that now she had a starting point from which to work where he was concerned.

Feeling decidedly upbeat, having finished the bottle of wine between them, they all trooped out. 'Any more of that wine and we'd have needed a map to get to the mess hall,' Pearl said. Again they all laughed. This was going to be a great place.

After a very good supper, again simple but well cooked, Signy slipped out of the mess hut to go for a walk by herself. It was already dusk, a lot cooler than during the day, with a moistness in the air, so that she draped the wide wool scarf that she'd brought with her around her shoulders, pulling it close. The need to be alone for a

while was paramount, as was the need to clear the image
of Simon from her mind.

She took a direction that she hadn't taken before, a
narrow concrete path than ran around the edge of the
camp, away from the mess and the residential huts. Some
of the other buildings looked as though they had originally
been drill halls, while some seemed to be divided up into
administrative offices. This camp was used for confer-
ences and other purposes, so she'd heard. World Aid
Doctors couldn't afford to keep such a place solely for
themselves—the place was subsidized by various levels
of government. It was an interesting place, and she looked
around her curiously.

It was good to feel the cool, refreshing air on her face,
to look up to see the pale grey of the evening sky, the
dark, tall, mysterious trees of the forest over to her left.

'Signy!' A voice spoke just behind her.

'Ah!' she gasped in alarm, having felt that she was
alone. Dan was on the path behind her, his tall figure just
visible in the gloom. 'Dr Blake, you…you frightened me.'

'Sorry. I guess I should have coughed or something,'
he said apologetically, coming up to her.

His presence bothered her, although she couldn't at that
moment analyse all the reasons why, and she had wanted
to be alone. It was at least partly because they'd been
discussing him before dinner. Also, there was a powerful,
understated masculinity about him and unlike Max
Seaton, he seemed unaware of its effect…even though he
wasn't her type, Signy reminded herself.

'I was rather hoping to be alone for a few minutes,' she
said candidly. 'I don't want to sound rude… It's just that
I…have things to think about. I suppose that's it.'

'Sorry again,' he said quietly, falling into step with her
as she began to walk slowly on again. He had changed

for dinner into stone-coloured cotton trousers that were casual yet somehow elegant on his spare frame, topped with an off-white, baggy shirt with the long sleeves rolled up. Signy looked at him covertly. At dinner her attention had been on Max, who had sat opposite her at the long table, although she had been all too aware of Dan and had deliberately not looked at him.

'I want to give you this handbook about earthquakes. It's put out specifically for this area, since you seem to be concerned about it,' he said, with no particular inflection in his voice, handing her a slim booklet. 'There should be at least one of these in each hut for you all to read. I guess you haven't seen it yet?'

'No. Thank you,' she said.

'It's a good idea to be aware, and prepared to a certain extent, but not to dwell on it,' he said. 'There's an earthquake preparation kit in each hut—bottled water, packaged food, a tent, battery radio, flashlight, matches, that sort of thing.'

'I see,' she said. At some point she had to broach the subject with him of whether he was the R.D.H. Blake she had heard about in Africa. The uncertainty of that unanswered question was making her increasingly agitated in his presence.

They walked on slowly, the scents of the forest around them. Signy sighed inwardly, very aware of the man at her side invading her privacy.

'Would you like me to go?' he said softly.

'No…no, it's all right,' she said, her face flushing with embarrassment.

'Grudging,' he commented, a smile in his voice. 'Definitely grudging.'

She glanced at him quickly but couldn't discern his expression in the dusk. 'It's my turn to apologize now,' she said. 'Sorry if I sound bad-tempered. It's just that I have a lot on my mind, which doesn't have to do with here and now.'

'Yes, I know,' he said. 'That's partly why you're here. Do you want to talk about it?'

Signy stopped on the pathway and turned to look at him. 'No!' she said emphatically, spitting out the word. 'You know, I'm sick and tired of people asking me that question, and I think the other nurses here are sick of it, too. I think when we talk, we'll talk to each other, or we'll do it when we're ready, not when we're being prompted. I know you mean well, so do those other professional listeners, but we have to be ready to talk.'

'I realize that, Signy,' he said seriously, looking down at her.

'Do you? It's mostly people who haven't themselves been anywhere other than a cosy office who ask that question...back and forth every day from cosy home to cosy office. I think that we who have been out to dangerous places are a curiosity to them. They have degrees in psychology, or something like that, and try to categorize you on a certain scale of norms that they were taught at university, to fit you into a stereotyped scheme that takes no account of you as an individual...'

'I don't think I come into that category,' he said.

'Perhaps not. It just sounds that way.'

'Signy, don't,' he said gently. He reached out and caught her arm, his fingers warm on her bare skin.

She tried to pull away but he held her forearm firmly in his grasp. 'Why not?' she demanded. 'It's true, isn't it?'

'As I said, not of me, I hope. I do know what you mean. We don't employ people with psychology degrees. We mainly have people who've been in dangerous and demanding situations themselves, not theorists,' he said.

It was the warmth of his hand, Signy decided, that made her feel vulnerable in his presence. 'They think they know everything,' she went on. 'It's so…so patronizing.'

'I agree,' he said.

'Then why are you asking me?'

'A simple sense that you might want to talk to someone,' he said. 'No strings attached, no particular agenda. Come on, let's walk.' His hand slid down her forearm to grasp her hand and pull her gently with him as he started to walk again.

Quickly she jerked her hand away, because she was beginning to find his touch comforting. Not that it mattered really. She told herself, somewhat grimly, that he wasn't a man to whom she could be attracted in a romantic sense, an anomalous man belonging to two countries, a mystery that she didn't care to fathom in the short time that was available to her. Although he was in some ways English and thus familiar, there was an alien quality to him. At any other time she might have welcomed that difference, but now she wasn't sure that she wanted to expend the mental energy.

'There is something you can tell me,' she said, making up her mind quickly and forcing the words out. 'Does the name Dominic Fraser mean anything to you? Dr Dominic Fraser?' As she asked the question she realized how angry she had been, as well as filled with grief, from the time that she'd heard about Dominic's fate. Up to now, the mourning had largely masked that anger.

'No,' he said, 'I don't think it does.'

'You are the R.D.H. Blake who was in Africa at the time we pulled out of Somalia?' she went on. 'I don't think there could be two people with those initials.'

They had stopped again and were facing each other. 'I was there at that time, briefly,' he said. 'I certainly didn't meet you before, and I didn't know a Dominic Fraser.'

'That's odd,' she said, rushing on, 'because we got a message from you at our medical station, telling us to pull out. It was brought by two people in a truck from World Aid Doctors. We had to pack up there and then and get into the truck. One of our party, Dr Fraser, was away at the time, trying to link up with some UN workers. Doesn't that mean anything to you?'

'What was the name of the medical station?' he asked quietly.

'It was at a small refugee crossing, a place called Lassi Ahmed,' she said. 'Mostly people only passed through. They stayed long enough to get some treatment, and then kept moving.'

'It rings a bell,' he said. 'Not far from the Kenyan border?'

'Yes, you could say that,' she said tightly. 'Far enough, though, when you're trying to get out.'

'If I sent a directive for you to get out,' he said, 'it would have come from someone else in the organization. I would have just been passing on a message from higher up the line, organizing a truck for the evacuation. I didn't have any decision-making power. When it's time to get out, you have to move in a hurry.'

Signy swallowed, trying to dispel the lump of emotion in her throat.

'I assume that this Dr Fraser didn't make it out?' he asked dryly, quietly.

'No...he didn't make it.'

'Am I to understand that you're somehow blaming me for that?' he asked.

'I...I don't know what to think,' she said, her voice trembling.

'Believe me,' he gave a mirthless laugh, 'I didn't have that sort of power. I wasn't making the decisions to pull out. I would have been passing on a message from those who co-ordinate all the assignments. We advise people to get out, provide them with the means. If they choose not to do so, that's their decision. At any one time we are overseeing quite a lot of different operations. I had my own work to do, as well as my own safety to think about.'

Obviously he remembered something about the operation, but not the details. Signy didn't want to tell him that not only had Dominic been missing, she herself had chosen not to take the truck with the others, had decided to stay for two more days to wait for Dominic. It had been a calculated risk...

For moments they stood looking at each other in the dusk, then he touched her arm lightly. 'Come on, let's continue our walk,' he invited.

'The first time I went to Africa,' Dan said, after moments of strained silence, 'was with World Aid Doctors, when I was a third-year medical student. They sent me to South Africa, an emergency clinic near a black township. It was supposed to be relatively safe, suitable for an inexperienced guy like myself. There were a lot of tensions, racial and otherwise. It was my job to mop up after riots and the like. I can't find adequate words to describe the things that I saw. There was also the knowledge that you would patch someone up, fight for their life, then they would go out and get injured again in a similar way.'

'Yes...I think I can picture it,' Signy said. 'I know that I don't have a monopoly on angst. It's just that one feels one does.'

They walked on in silence, the path having brought

them to an area where a high chain-link fence enclosed the grounds of the camp, making a very definite demarcation line between the forest and the man-made dwelling place. An attempt had been made to cultivate the area inside the fence, with flower-beds here and there and with low shrubs that wouldn't be a threat in the event of a forest fire.

'One of the reasons we can't talk about things,' Dan went on quietly, 'is that we can't make sense of what has happened, and we want desperately to make sense of it—make sense of human behaviour. Later we come to see that talking to others who have had the same experiences is cathartic, even if there is no logic to what has taken place.'

'I suppose that's it,' Signy said. When his arm accidentally brushed hers as they walked along the narrow path she had a sense of wanting to cry, her emotions very close to the surface, as though the human contact gave her permission to let go when she had spent so long holding herself in check, bearing up.

Maybe that was what Dan intended. She didn't like the idea that she could be somehow an experiment for him, part of the job he was doing. Instinctively she didn't think that was the case, yet she moved to the edge of the path away from him.

'But you want to go back to the same kind of work?' he asked.

'Yes, I think so. But this time I don't want to be quite so green, so naïve. I want to be as prepared as I can possibly be, and to have some choice about where I go, if I can. Maybe I won't go back to Africa…not for a long time, anyway.'

'We can only go where we're wanted. We can't impose ourselves. This is no do-gooder organization. You learn humility, a certain cynicism, I think,' he said. 'You have to have your feet very firmly on the ground. Idealism is great, but it has to be tempered with realism, a necessary protection for oneself.'

Signy remained silent, still not caring to tell him that she hadn't taken the truck out when it had come to rescue them. Very forcefully, a renewed realization hit her that she was very lucky to be alive. They walked on slowly. In spite of their topic of conversation, there was a magical quality in the air, a rich mellowness, even though the air had cooled with the going down of the sun. A wind from the ocean rustled the tops of the trees, yet they were largely sheltered from it.

She felt the oddity of walking here, as though for a regular evening stroll, with a man for whom she felt nothing of significance emotionally, other than wariness, a man she hadn't known before that morning. Well, she would resist his efforts to categorize her, if that was what he might be trying to do.

'What makes you want to go on?' he said.

'Oh…to give up now, after what I've endured, would somehow betray the others, who showed such courage and dedication in their work.' She had been going to say that it would somehow betray Dominic, but she bit the words back. Maybe Dan had already surmised the rest of her story, but she wasn't ready to confide in him further. Neither was she ready to tell him that for a long time afterwards she had felt as though she were sleep-walking, just going through the motions of being alive. Obsessively she had thought of Dominic, how they'd worked together, all that he'd ever said to her, how they'd shared jokes…she and the other nurses and doctors.

Of course, she hadn't loved him in the way that she'd loved Simon. No, they had been colleagues who had worked very closely together and had become close emotionally because of it. There had been no romance, more a fierce sense of loyalty.

The path eventually curved back towards the centre. As they made the turn, Dan stopped, touching her arm again. 'There's something else I want to say to you, Signy,' he said, 'something that isn't easy to say.'

She waited.

'Be careful of Max Seaton,' he said.

The unexpected warning brought a renewed flush to her face which she was very glad Dan couldn't see. His own face was a pale blur.

'Why?' she said. 'We're all mature women here.'

'He likes to make conquests,' Dan said. 'And here he has plenty of opportunity among women who are vulnerable in more ways than one.'

'Oh?' she said, antagonism making her tart. 'And what ways are those, Dr Blake?'

'I don't have to spell it out to you, Signy,' he said quietly.

'I think we can look after ourselves in that regard,' she said, 'thank you very much. So what if a woman wants, and chooses, to have a friendship—or an affair—with a very attractive and nice man? Maybe some of them here do.'

'Perhaps,' he said. 'Not wise.'

'As for me,' she said, 'there have been two men in my recent past whom I've loved very much. You don't suddenly stop loving someone because you don't have them in your life in the same way, or see them.'

'I know,' he said.

'I'm not actively looking for someone, so I don't think you need to warn me,' she said. It wasn't strictly true that she had loved both men in the way that this man was talking about; she hadn't loved Dominic in the way that she had loved Simon. Dominic had been more like a brother, the relationship growing in the face of shared tensions and work.

Irritatingly, Dan said nothing.

'This is an odd conversation to be having when you don't know me, when we just met this morning,' she commented.

'As I said before, we don't have much time. Sometimes we get into situations when we're very lonely, especially when we're a long way from home,' he said. 'Situations that aren't ultimately good for us, with no possibility of permanence. It's the loneliness speaking. We're particularly vulnerable when we're on an assignment. It's understandable. We all do it.'

'Even you?' she said.

'Even me.'

'I don't need a lecture,' she said bluntly. 'Sometimes we don't want permanence. I think I'm a pretty good judge of character and motives.' Had that, in fact, been true with Simon? The thought nagged at her, as well as the memory of her carefree youth, unheeding in many ways. Well, she was older now, perhaps wiser.

'That's good,' he said.

'Do you make conquests among vulnerable women, Dr Blake?' she asked, hearing the antagonism in her own voice. She wanted to equalize the situation, where she wasn't the one answering all the questions.

For a long moment he said nothing, just looked at her, so that she thought he was not going to answer.

'I prefer to let nature take its course.' he said. 'Fifty-fifty.'

They walked back in a somewhat strained silence—at least, she felt strained. As they got closer to the central

area they could hear music playing in the mess hall.
'Someone must have started an impromptu party,' Dan
said. 'That often happens.'

As they got closer into the lighted area, he turned to
her and gave a bow. 'Will you favour me with the pleasure of this dance, Ms Clover?'

Stiff with an antagonism that she couldn't understand,
Signy none the less conceded that Dan had been straight-
forward with her, had in many ways been kind. Without
speaking, she nodded an assent.

Inside the mess the lights were dim. A stereo was playing soft music. There were not quite enough men to go
round, although Signy saw a few other men she hadn't
met before, who presumably worked at the camp and on
the island in maintenance, the kitchens, forestry and other
areas. Jock McGregor was there.

Dan drew her into his arms, a look of irony on his face
as she failed to relax. 'You can pretend to be enjoying
yourself,' he said, bending his head down to her, 'then
maybe you'll find that you really are.'

They moved slowly in time to the music in a small
space that had been cleared in the centre of the large,
utilitarian room.

Terri, in Max's arms, waved to her, and she began to
relax. Dan held her lightly but firmly against his lean,
muscular body as they danced, the rhythm coming easily
and naturally to him, so it seemed to her. He was a man
of surprises. Certainly he wasn't as mixed up as she felt.

Again she had a feeling of dissonance. How strange it
seemed that in such a short time she should be halfway
around the world, dancing in a disused military base in
the middle of an island forest, with a man she had just
met that morning. Yet that was the nature of the work that

she had chosen to do. Events were taking place faster than her mind could keep up with them.

Inevitably she eventually relaxed as the music changed several times, and she was surprised to find that she was so close to Dan that she could feel the heat of his body through the thin cotton of her blouse. Hastily she jerked back from him.

'Would you like a drink?' Dan queried, no doubt sensing her withdrawal. 'A Coke, or something?' There was a light of amusement in his eyes. 'And I'm going to spread myself around.'

'Mmm…yes…thanks,' she mumbled.

As Dan moved away from her through the small crowd, Signy felt herself turned round as though she were as light as a feather and drawn into the arms of Max Seaton. 'I've been waiting for this,' he said huskily. 'I thought I was never going to get a look-in.' He was laughing down at her, his eyes alight with open admiration.

'Oh?' she said, thinking again how good-looking he was, how apparently sure of himself. Yet she felt unmoved, apart from a mild curiosity about him.

When the music stopped they were close to the door, manoeuvred there, Signy suspected, by Max.

'Shall we go out for a little air?' he said.

'I've just had a lot of air.' She laughed. 'And Dan was getting me a drink.' With that, she eased herself away from him. 'You have to spread yourself around, Dr Seaton, since there aren't enough men.'

He shrugged. 'Maybe,' he said. 'You should tell that to the worthy Dan.'

The word 'worthy', applied to Dan, was oddly jarring to her, a subtle put-down, she felt. It implied that he was a good man, but a bit of a bumpkin. That certainly didn't apply to Dan, whom she felt instinctively to be a complex man, sophisticated in an understated way, capable of great surprises. How she knew all that she couldn't have said at that moment. Indeed, she surprised herself by coming to his defence, if only in her own mind, in spite of her underlying antagonism.

'Well, excuse me,' she said, a little awkwardly.

Dan was standing at the counter near the kitchen hatch that was used as a bar, surrounded by some of the other nurses with whom he was in conversation. There was a smile on his face as he talked animatedly to them. If Signy had expected him to be hanging around, waiting for her, she was disabused. Instead, he calmly turned round to pick up a full glass from the bar and hand it to her.

'Your drink, Ms Clover,' he said. 'I rather think that most of the fizz has gone out of it.'

'Thank you,' she said stiffly. Somehow she felt there was a hidden meaning in his words.

CHAPTER THREE

SUNDAY was truly a day of rest. Signy got up late, dressed casually and went for a late breakfast which, she found when she got to the mess hall, was combined with brunch until half past two in the afternoon. As she left her own hut, she appreciated the printed sign on the door that separated the sitting room from the passage that led to the sleeping rooms, which said, ABSOLUTE QUIET, PLEASE.

She'd thought last night that she wouldn't sleep, as so many thoughts had been churning through her head, but she had, in fact, slept heavily.

Connie and Pearl, as well as two other nurses, were having breakfast. 'Hello,' Signy greeted them.

'Hi,' Connie said. 'Come and join us.'

After getting herself coffee, a croissant and some fruit salad, Signy sat down at the table.

'This is great Indian summer weather, as we call it out here,' Connie said. 'Have you got plans for the day, Signy? Some of us were thinking of going for a walk. Are you game?'

'I'd love to,' Signy said. 'First of all I've got to set up my laptop and send a few e-mails to family and friends to let them know I got here safely. My mother won't sleep until she knows I'm all right. I've also got to think about jobs, earning a living between assignments. I brought some journals with me to go through.'

'Same here,' Pearl said. 'I guess we chose the wrong outfit with this World Aid business, as far as our families are concerned. They know we're OK in Canada, although my family knows all about grizzly bears. I've said there won't be any where I'm going, which I think is a lie.'

'I've stopped telling people exactly where I'm being sent if there's more than average danger,' Connie said. 'I find it's easier on them and on me. But I must be at least fifteen years older than you two, so it's a bit different for me. I have a son who's seventeen—he stays with my mother when I'm on an overseas job. He's secretly proud of me, I think. These days I'm trying not to go anywhere too dangerous. Most of the time I just work here in a city hospital. Give me an earthquake, a landslide, a volcanic eruption or a hurricane, rather than any place where there's civil unrest or an outbreak of something awful like the Ebola virus.'

They talked, tentatively revealing a few details of their lives.

'We've been given our assignments already for two weeks from tomorrow—there's a list up on that notice-board over there,' Pearl said to Signy, pointing to a large cork-board near the door. 'All of us from Moose Head are going to be with Dan Blake, going by float plane to that little place up the BC coast that Connie was telling us about earlier, Brookes Landing.'

'It started off as a logging camp years ago,' Connie chipped in. 'It has a community hospital, so we'll be going there to observe and do various things. We have to be ready to leave by seven-thirty at the float-plane dock.'

'That sounds intriguing,' Signy said, then went over to the noticeboard to see for herself, feeling a stab of excitement tinged with a certain nervousness that always assailed her at the beginning of a new assignment, even though this was merely a training session.

'Well,' she commented, seating herself at the table again, 'we've got two weeks to get to know something about the place. It's not like going off somewhere at a moment's notice.'

'You can say that again.' Connie smiled. 'It will be a piece of cake.'

The next two weeks of lectures, orientation and training went by quickly and enjoyably, for the most part. Visiting lecturers came to the island to talk to the group. Dan Blake and Max Seaton were there some of the time, although they had to leave at times to fulfil their commitments to their regular professional jobs on the mainland.

Dan didn't single her out, Signy was relieved to find, during that time. Over the two weeks she read the booklet that he had given her about earthquakes. The first line in the book was sobering. 'In the event of an earthquake, consider yourself on your own, and pre-plan for that eventuality,' it said. It then went on to tell you how to pre-plan, then what to do when the event happened, what to expect. First, you took care of yourself, because no one else would; then you helped those immediately around you, if you were capable of doing so. After that you assisted your neighbours, then you would search for family members if they weren't in your area. One had to be prepared for the probability that all or most emergency and community services would either break down or be severely inadequate. In other words, one couldn't expect help.

Although plagued now and then by bad dreams, Signy found that they were fewer than they had been in England, perhaps because she was surrounded by colleagues here who had shared similar experiences. There was a collective empathy that was reassuring.

There were seven people in the plane, including the pilot, on Monday morning two weeks later—the four nurses from Moose Head hut, plus Dan and Max who had both been on the island on the Sunday. This time there was a pilot they hadn't met before, whose permanent job was flying planes, so Max informed them when they were all seated.

It was a beautiful day, with the sun shining, the air clear and crisp, the sky and sea a pristine blue, contrasting dramatically with the grey rocks on the shoreline of the island and the dark green of the towering conifers. The plane rose into the air and headed northeast, then turned due north when the coast of the mainland came into view, taking them to Brookes Landing. Over the past two weeks they had all studied a detailed map to orientate themselves to where they were going and to understand the lie of the land and islands in between. The other eight nurses were being taken by boat, accompanied by Jock, to some of the other islands where there were medical clinics. It was their intention to observe how these clinics were set up and how they were run on a day-to-day basis.

Signy looked out of the window at the seascape and landscape beneath her, conscious at the same time that Max sat behind her. She felt as though his glance were boring into the back of her neck. For some reason, it seemed he had singled her out for special attention, or maybe he just latched onto anyone who was within his orbit.

Once she looked up ahead to see Dan glancing back briefly, his eyes meeting hers with what she could only term a sardonic expression. Most of the time he was chatting to Terri, who was sitting behind him.

'You'll no doubt find Brookes Landing a prosaic little place,' Max said, as Signy half turned round in her seat to look at him as he spoke, piqued that Dan should see fit to pass judgement and issue warnings about this man, as though she were a child and couldn't decide for herself. She supposed his intentions were good—she just didn't know. By now she should be able to take care of herself. Maybe someone should warn her about Dan, she thought as she glanced back at him, now chatting to Connie and Pearl, having to talk loudly above the noise of the plane engine. Not that she was about to get involved with Dan Blake in any way...

'How long have you been a surgeon at Brookes Landing?' she asked Max.

'Quite a few years,' he said. 'There and other small places. I travel round a lot. At Brookes Landing we do something of everything in the way of surgery, as long as we feel we can cope with it. There's a fair amount of trauma, although we have a good service for moving patients out to Vancouver if we get something we can't cope with.'

Signy nodded in commiseration, suspecting that Max wasn't making idle conversation to pass the time. Everything he was telling her, everything he was showing her from the window, was part of the orientation and training process. They were passing over other small islands.

There was something about being in a strange place, she thought, that helped you to see yourself and your concerns from the outside, to see yourself as others might see you to a certain extent. It made some of those concerns seem petty.

Brookes Landing turned out to be not quite big enough for a town—more a large, scattered village of small wood-frame houses that were built over a series of hills, beginning not far from the ocean. On the far side, where the houses ended, there was a large cleared area, before the forest began. The nurses could see all that from the air as they came in to land on the water.

They trooped up from the dock to a terminus building that was basic in the extreme. 'We have to check in,' Max said, speaking to the nurses. 'They like to know who's here in the community, especially the whereabouts of doctors and nurses. We have a mini-van parked here, which belongs to the hospital.'

'While Max checks us in,' Dan said, 'we'll get into the van.'

'This looks like a frontier town,' Pearl remarked, with calm understatement.

'It's cut off,' Dan said. 'The roads don't go anywhere after the first few miles. There are a lot of logging roads—tracks really. You travel by plane and boat.'

They all got into the van, and when Max joined them they drove off slowly up a hill, with Dan driving. A light rain began to fall. Looking back towards the ocean, Signy saw that in the short time that they had been there a thin grey mist had come up over the water.

The four nurses looked around them avidly, not saying much. The remoteness of the place, the feeling of being cut off, with the brooding forest in the background, was sobering to them. Signy felt as though she were driving through a Christmas card scene, with conifers here and there and the rather quaint small wooden houses. There were few people on the narrow streets. She saw a harbour where boats were moored, then a general store and post office, where a man stood outside and waved as they went by.

'That's my cabin,' Dan said, pointing to what Signy thought of as a large shack, a wooden structure covered with unpainted wood siding, the roof covered with cedar shingles. It had a verandah over the front door, where she could just read a sign as they drove by which said HERON COTTAGE.

'Is this your home, Dr Blake?' Connie asked politely, yet unable to keep a slightly incredulous note out of her voice.

'Only when I have to be in Brookes Landing,' he said. 'I have a place in the city.'

The others said nothing, just exchanged glances, wondering how they themselves would fare in this rather wild place.

The hospital was one of the few concrete buildings in the village, a single-storey, rather spread-out building, set among trees and gardens. 'This hospital serves other communities up the coast,' Max said as he pushed open the main doors to the central part of the building and they all trooped in ahead of him, 'as well as people who live out in the bush nearer to the logging camps.'

'Ah, Dr Blake! Dr Seaton!' A middle-aged nurse stood behind a reception desk in the main hallway, obviously delighted to see the two doctors. 'And you've brought some helping hands with you! That's just great.'

Signy noted that the nurse greeted Dan first, even though Max had been slightly ahead of them all. Perhaps, she thought, it was because Dan had a house in the community, that he spent more time there. Max had told them that he had a room in the hospital when he needed to stay there to look after his pre-op and post-op patients.

'Go into the kitchen,' the nurse went on, smiling a welcome to them all. 'Get yourselves a bit of lunch. There should be someone there who can help you.'

'Thanks, Maggie,' Dan said. 'Great to see you looking so good.'

The kitchen was for the preparation of food for both patients and staff. They were directed to help themselves to food that was already cooked, then to carry it into the adjoining staff dining room.

'Well,' Terri said to the other nurses when they were seated, 'this hospital's a cute little place. I wouldn't mind doing a short stint here.'

'That's what you're going to be doing,' Dan said, having overheard her remark. 'After lunch you, Terri, and you, Pearl, will go to the operating rooms with Max. He has a few surgical procedures to do there. Connie and Signy, you will be with me. I have some house calls to make out in the sticks.'

A sharp disappointment assailed Signy, which she strove to control, realizing that she had somehow taken it for granted that she would spend time with Max who, in spite of his gorgeous appearance, seemed less complex than Dan, and was less fraught with emotional nuances.

A look of pleasure lit up Terri's face. 'Just what I need,' she said.

'The sticks?' Signy said, frowning at Dan.

'Out in the backwoods,' he said. 'We have all-terrain vehicles and we go on logging roads. I have a pregnant woman out there and a man who has cancer of the colon. There isn't any more we can do for him because he's decided that he doesn't want any more chemotherapy but wants to stay out in the woods with his wife. He knows he can come into the hospital here any time if he changes his mind.'

'Doesn't that make a lot of work for you?' Terri queried.

Dan shrugged, his face serious. 'Not really. That's where he wants to be, so we must respect that. Mainly it makes work for the nurses who go in to see him more than I do, and his wife, of course. We do what we can for him. If he were here in the hospital his wife couldn't be with him all the time, which is what they both want…at least, for now.'

'What about the pregnant woman?' Connie asked. 'Is it her first baby?'

'No, it's her third,' Dan said. 'She's agreed to come into hospital at the first sign of labour, or a week before the baby's due, whichever comes first, or alternatively at the first sign of any trouble. I tell my pregnant patients that I'll accommodate their wishes as much as I can, but if they won't ultimately accept my professional advice from the outset, I won't take them on.'

They were on the road again not long after lunch, riding in a well-worn Jeep, with Dan driving and Connie beside him. Signy sat in the back. It was where she preferred to be at that moment. Really, she wasn't sure why she felt tense in Dan's presence. Perhaps it was because he was astute, at ease with himself and this environment, not trying to impress anyone, while she felt somewhat like a fish out of water, even though what she was witnessing was fascinating in many ways.

They had stopped at Heron Cottage to pick up some medical equipment, then had gone on past Dan's cabin. Although the rain had stopped, the air was heavy with moisture, while the mountains in the distance and some of the closer hills that they had seen earlier were now completely hidden by dense, low cloud.

'This is one of the logging roads I was telling you about,' Dan explained as he drove carefully along a wide lane. 'Huge trucks used to come along here to bring logs from the forest down to the water, where they were floated down to a saw-mill. It used to be done with horses in the old days. Now there isn't any logging in this particular spot—all the suitable trees have been used up. The people in Brookes Landing maintain the roads because people live along here now.'

He turned his head to look at Signy. 'Ever seen anything like this, Signy?' he said, his tone, slightly teasing, implying that she probably had never seen anything as rugged as this in her life.

'It's a bit like parts of Kent,' she said casually. Indeed, there were forests, albeit small, in parts of Kent and Sussex that she knew of. She didn't want him to think that she had spent her life pounding concrete pavements, or that this place had a monopoly on ruggedness and hardship.

Dan gave her an assessing look, before concentrating on the driving.

'Tell us more about this man with cancer of the colon, please,' Signy asked.

'His name's Felix George,' Dan said. 'He had a gut resection for the tumour some time ago. He had some chemotherapy because some of the local lymph nodes were involved. We thought he was clear, then recently he showed up with metastases in the liver.'

'Familiar story,' Connie commented. 'There should be more routine screening for colon cancer, since it's relatively common.'

'Yes, exactly,' Dan said. 'Felix started to lose weight, feel unwell, but didn't do anything about it until there was significant spread. He's been out of the province quite a bit, travelling, and didn't do as he was advised about frequent check-ups. Now he's back here for good and there's nothing we can do for him except make him comfortable, unless he decides that he wants further chemo. It may be too late for that, of course. It's very sad.'

Both Connie and Signy were silent. They had both met patients like the man being described. Maybe he'd decided that he didn't want to live in fear for his life all the time, and would just carry on as usual.

After driving along the lane, which twisted and turned, for quite a while, Dan brought the car to a halt at a road-side cabin. 'This belongs to a forest ranger,' he said, looking at Connie and Signy in turn. 'We have to walk a few yards up that track.' He pointed to a narrow path that disappeared among some conifers.

Signy watched him as he unfolded his long legs and got out of the vehicle in one lithe movement, then embarrassingly became aware that she was staring at him and that Connie was already out. Truth to tell, she couldn't make up her mind about him. Still seething from the shock she had felt at realizing that he had been in Africa at the same time that she had, she felt determined not to engage with him emotionally until she could find out more. It was easy to look for someone to blame, she knew that.

The first thing Dan unloaded from a zip-up bag was a shotgun. While Connie and Signy looked on silently, he quickly checked that the gun was loaded. 'This is for any unexpected encounters with wildlife,' he said. 'Cougars or bears.'

They put on their rain jackets, then between the three of them they carried Dan's bags of medical equipment, with him leading the way. 'Ah, it's good to walk!' Connie said, taking several very deep breaths. 'To breathe in the pure air, to be in silence so profound that one can almost hear it.'

'Yes,' Signy agreed appreciatively, doing the same thing. 'You sound so poetic, Connie. I don't know whether I could be so eloquent.'

'If you think that's eloquent,' Connie said with a smile, 'you should hear me when I'm bawling out a patient in an emergency department—you know, one of those obstreperous types.'

'Oh, we can all be pretty good at that,' Dan chipped in, and they all laughed companionably.

'I can see why we need hiking boots,' Signy said as they trudged on, looking at the rugged path that was liberally sprinkled with small, half-buried rocks.

'Talking of boots,' Dan said, 'it's the custom here to take your footwear off when you enter someone's house or cabin, however humble, to prevent dirt from getting tracked in, especially as there's so much rain here. It gets a bit tedious, I'm afraid.'

The residence of Felix George and his wife proved to be a modest bungalow made of wood in a beautiful setting of evergreen trees and grey rocks. Flower beds and a small vegetable plot had been carved out of the rather sparse soil. The three of them were breathing rather heavily by the time they had climbed the steps to the front porch, as the footpath had gone uphill.

'And I thought I was pretty fit,' Connie said ruefully.

A woman opened the door before they knocked. She was middle-aged with a weather-worn face, her wavy grey hair pulled behind her head in a ponytail. To Signy she looked like what she was—the wife of a very sick man, tired and anxious. Now her face creased in a welcoming smile. 'Dr Blake!' she said. 'I was hoping you'd come today. And you've brought visitors! That *is* nice. Come in.'

'Good to see you, Donna,' Dan said, smiling back.

Grudgingly, Signy admired Dan's ease and gentleness with people, his empathy and warmth. Yet he hadn't, so far, stepped out of line, hadn't become familiar. He'd remained professional, even when he'd had quizzed her on the ride to the camp and when he'd danced with her. In turn, people responded to him, she'd noticed.

'Meet two nurses who are with the World Aid Nurses programme,' he said to Donna George. 'I hope you and Felix don't mind if they're with me. I mentioned it last time. They're here to learn about community work.'

'No, that's great,' Donna said, shaking hands with Connie and Signy in turn. 'I really admire what you people do, going out to those places where no one else wants to go. I've read all about the work you do, and I do my bit here to raise money for the organization. In your case, it isn't a matter of where fools rush in, is it? Quite the opposite.'

'I like to think so,' Signy said, smiling, warmed by the other woman's greeting yet at the same time feeling a peculiar twinge of something like conscience.

Now she wasn't sure that she had always behaved and reacted in the most mature fashion when in danger. In the very short time that she had been in this part of the world, listening to the talks given by Dan, Max and others, she found herself thinking about her work experiences in a somewhat different light. No doubt, that was what they intended—the process had begun. Even though she had undergone a training before, this time it would be backed up by the invaluable practical experience that she had received in the field, which shed an entirely different light on any theoretical training. It was all part of the maturation process.

Dan had stepped over the threshold and was bending down to unlace his boots. 'How's Felix, Donna?' he asked quietly. 'Any change from last week?'

The woman hesitated slightly. 'I don't think so, really,' she answered quietly. 'At least, not physically. I do think he might be a little depressed... More so than he was before. He sometimes takes the painkillers you left for him. He's not a man to complain, you see, so I'm wondering if he might be in more pain than he's letting on—or just depressed. I think it's that.'

'I see,' Dan said. 'He's a bit down, is he?'

'Yes, he just gets very quiet. Nothing you could really put your finger on. I've been wondering if he would be better off with some medication for his moods as well,' she went on. 'But the suggestion would have to come from you, I think, Dr Blake. I don't want him to know that I've been talking about that behind his back...he's very sensitive that way...'

Signy's heart went out to this woman, this tired, loving woman who was nursing a seriously ill man in an isolated place. As she looked around her she could see that they at least had electricity, weren't cut off from that point of view. As far as she could see, they had all the modern conveniences.

'I'll talk to him,' Dan said, a warm, reassuring note in his voice that moved Signy to a further somewhat reluctant empathy with him and the work he was called upon to do here.

'Thanks, I'd appreciate it,' Donna said, sounding relieved.

Glancing quickly at Connie as they followed the woman into the house, Signy sensed that she, too, had the impression that Donna was close to breaking point, that at the drop of a hat she would burst into tears. They also sensed that she was a strong, sensible, capable woman, who would go on here as long as she possibly could, if that was what her husband wanted, but that she would make the decision to move him out to hospital if or when the situation warranted it.

Their patient was sitting beside a desk in a small side

room off the kitchen, through which they passed. He faced a large picture window which gave him a view of wilderness, apparently untouched by human hand. Beautiful conifers, in varying shades of green, dotted a rock-strewn hillside, where shrubs and grasses also grew in profusion. As they entered, he turned his eyes away from it, as though reluctantly.

On the large desk, which took up most of the space in the room, Signy saw a computer and printer, a fax machine and two telephones. The computer was switched on. At least this man and his wife weren't isolated from the local community, or from the world, as far as communication was concerned. They could call for help and expect to get it. Those gadgets put a whole new interpretation on the concept. That wasn't how it had been for her and her colleagues in Africa…not for Dominic.

As Felix looked at them, Signy could see that the conjunctiva of his eyes had a faint yellowish tinge. This was evident in the colour of his skin also, although barely, so that to the unpractised observer it could appear as the unhealthy pallor of a chronically sick man. To her, it signified liver disease.

'Well, Dan,' he said, smiling, 'it's good to see you again.' He was a big man, well over six feet tall, on whom the flesh hung loosely, as though he had lost a lot of weight, and his cheeks were hollow, his eyes dull.

When introductions had been made, and it had been ascertained that Felix didn't object to having two visiting nurses review his case, Donna excused herself to make coffee. As Signy seated herself in an offered chair, she suspected that the woman couldn't bear to listen to her husband go over his symptoms once again, to perhaps have to admit that he was deteriorating.

The two nurses listened and watched unobtrusively

while Dan talked to the man. He asked him gently about his mental state and suggested a mood-elevating drug, to which Felix agreed. Then they helped while Dan took blood samples.

'This computer is a godsend,' the man said, 'so is the fax. I'm in constant touch with anyone I want to be in touch with, including old friends I haven't actually seen for many years. They all take time to send me messages. It means a lot, you know.'

Dan chatted to him about non-medical matters as he completed the taking of blood samples and filled in requisition forms for the hospital lab.

'I'd like to examine you, Felix,' Dan said. 'The usual.'

'All right.'

While they all shifted to make room, their patient moved over to a narrow day-bed that was against a wall in the room, where he obviously took a nap when he felt the need. Dan listened to his heart and lungs with a stethoscope, took his blood pressure, then gently palpated his abdomen. Both Connie and Signy, with the patient's permission, palpated the abdomen also, feeling the irregular shape of the liver that had tumours in it.

Later, they drank coffee in the kitchen, while conversation ranged over topics of local concern to take the focus away from the import of the sickness. Then Dan left some containers of drugs that he had brought with him.

Soon they were taking their leave, setting off down the path, which would be an easier trek on the way back, towards the forest ranger's hut. At a bend in the path they turned to wave back at Donna and Felix, who stood at the door to see them off.

'That's very sad,' Connie commented when they were out of sight and earshot of the house. 'Tempered by the

fact that he can be at home where he wants to be, with
all his electronic gadgets.'

'Yes…he enjoys those things, as well as the scenery,'
Dan agreed, with just a hint of tiredness in his voice to
indicate that the visit had moved him more than his calm
professional demeanour had indicated while he'd been ex-
amining the patient. He stopped on the path. 'We may as
well review the case here. I assume that you both felt the
liver tumours and noted that he had some abdominal ascites?'

'Yes.' Signy nodded in agreement. There had been
fluid—ascites—in the abdominal cavity, indicating that
the liver tumours had grown to a size that was obstructing
blood and lymph vessels, impeding the drainage of fluid.
'You're going to keep him at home?'

'As I said, it's up to him, to a point…he knows that,'
Dan answered. 'It's his decision, or his wife's decision if
she can't cope any more. If they turn the decision over to
me, then I'll make it. Prior to that, I'll advise them, of
course. We have to fine-tune his drugs to make sure he's
comfortable. There's someone going in every day right
now—a community nurse.'

They trudged on down the path, the images of the people they had just left and thoughts about the prognosis
vying with the compelling landscape around them. 'Nature seems so powerful here, doesn't it?' Signy blurted
out. 'One feels overwhelmed by it. It's as though…it's as
though man doesn't really have much of a chance.'

'Yes,' Connie said. 'You have to know and respect nature here, otherwise it will get you, take you by surprise.
But the winters are reasonable here, almost benign, com-
pared with a lot of places in this country.'

'I'm getting a sense of that,' Signy said. 'And there
isn't much history here, as we know it.'

'True,' Dan said. 'I often think that we humans sit uneasily on the landscape.'

'I like the way you put that,' she said.

'The history belongs to geology, the flora and fauna,' Connie said.

'Not like Kent after all,' Dan said dryly, looking sideways at Signy with a slight raising of his eyebrows.

'No...perhaps not,' Signy said, flushing slightly. 'There are a few poisonous snakes here and there.'

'Look,' he said, pointing up at two very large birds that suddenly soared above their heads, crossing their path, majestic and silent. 'Those are eagles—bald eagles, so called because of the white head in contrast with the black body. From a distance they look bald.'

'They're magnificent,' Signy breathed, watching the birds glide effortlessly and gracefully to near the top of a very tall conifer to settle themselves on a branch. 'They belong here. We don't.'

'Speak for yourself,' Connie said.

Back at the car, Dan reached in for a pair of binoculars and trained them on the two immobile birds in the distant tree. 'Take a look,' he said, handing the binoculars to Signy and standing beside her. 'They look even better close up.'

Focusing the glasses on the head of one of the birds, Signy could see the thick white feathers of the head that contrasted with the darker body. The tail feathers, too, were white. The fierce, proud head, the yellow, watchful eyes that seemed to see everything at once in the forest around, the hooked beak, all filled her vision. She could also see the talons that grasped the branch of the tree.

'It's wonderful,' she whispered, as though the bird might be disturbed by her words. 'I've never seen a bird like that. It's somehow...magical.' She found herself smiling up at Dan, her antagonism momentarily forgotten. When he smiled back at her she felt a very rare moment of total empathy, as though the world had shifted for a few seconds into a state of perfect synchronicity.

'Yes, it often seems that way,' he said.

His words broke what seemed like a strange, momentary spell, and she looked away from him, automatically handing the binoculars to the other nurse. 'Have a look, Connie,' she offered.

When they had stowed their gear, Connie got into the back seat. 'You can have a chance to appreciate the views from the front seat, Signy,' she said.

Dan seemed aware of her reluctance to sit with him, and gave her a small, wry smile. They drove back part of the way they had come earlier, then branched off on another small, rutted track.

'My patient who's having the baby is along here,' he said. 'She had an ultrasound at the hospital recently, which shows that all is well so far. Many of the original immigrants to this part were from England and Scotland, her ancestors among them. Her name's Kathy Lahey, and she's thirty-four. Sometimes she comes up to the hospital, sometimes I see her here.'

The Lahey house was very similar to the Georges', made of wood covered with wood siding, the roof shingled with cedar. It was small and unassuming. After they had rung the doorbell, a woman appeared with two young children at her side who stared at them from the doorway.

'Oh, Dr Blake! Great to see you,' the woman said. 'It's good to have visitors.' She was short and slight, fair-haired, heavily pregnant.

Kathy was intrigued to be introduced to someone from England as her grandparents, she explained, had been emigrants from there. Many of their countrymen had cleared the land, built the communities here.

'You make me feel very welcome.' Signy smiled. 'I feel inspired to read more of the history.'

'It's not a very long history,' Kathy said. 'We're relative newcomers in the wilderness when you compare it with Europe.'

When a routine examination had been done, they all had another cup of coffee, while the two children, about seven and five years old, Signy guessed, looked on shyly.

'The ultrasound is normal,' Dan explained.

'Thank God for that,' Kathy said. 'I think this will be my last baby. Three's about all I can handle.'

As they were taking their leave, Dan's cellphone shrilled, breaking incongruously into the silence of the land that surrounded the isolated dwelling.

'Ah, the voice of the future,' Connie commented, while Dan answered it.

'Dan Blake here,' he said, as they paused at the bottom of the house steps, while Connie and Signy shouldered the bags of equipment. He listened, frowning, his face serious, concentrated. 'Yes… How bad is it? Right… Well, we're leaving here now on our way back. I can be there.'

The two nurses waited expectantly. 'Bad news, Dr Blake?' Connie said.

'Yes. Let's get going,' Dan said, starting off back to the vehicle, reaching to relieve them of some of the equipment as they went. 'It looks as though we might not get back to Kelp Island tonight. They need help at the hospital, from all of us. Two men were attacked by a cougar farther up the coast, and they've been brought here by plane. They're at the hospital now.'

'Oh, heck,' Connie said. 'What sort of a state are they in?'

Signy remained silent as they stowed the bags quickly in the car and got in themselves. She wasn't exactly sure what a cougar was, and didn't want to appear ignorant. She knew that there were wild coyotes, fox-like creatures, in the province that attacked pets and small dogs in human communities.

'They've lost blood from multiple lacerations, but fortunately no damaged eyes or mutilation of faces, just a lot of claw marks, apparently, from being mauled,' Dan said tersely as he backed the vehicle out of the parking space and turned around to make their exit. 'Unfortunately, the only staff surgeon in the place is in the middle of something, so Max and I are going to have to deal with those two cases in the operating room. There's a shortage of nurses in the OR as well, so I think that you two will have to help. If you want to, that is.'

'Yes, of course,' Connie said. 'Just as well we've got interim employee status here, isn't it?'

'How about you, Signy?' Dan turned an enquiring look on her.

'Yes.' Signy echoed her assent, feeling shocked by what had happened.

'Yes, of course.' She added rather hesitantly, 'I'm not quite sure what a cougar is.'

'A big cat,' Connie said.

'With very big teeth,' Dan added, 'and very sharp claws.'

'Is this a common occurrence?' Signy said, trying to picture it and failing.

'It's rare that they attack humans,' he said.

Sitting next to him, Signy looked quickly at his serious profile, then away again, as he concentrated on the driving. As she was observing him in his work here, she could imagine what he would be like working with World Aid Doctors, getting a sense that he would be very careful about the decisions he made. Again, she began to feel the glimmerings of some serious unease about some of the decisions she herself had made…

CHAPTER FOUR

'WE COULD really use a plastic surgeon here,' Dan said very quietly to Signy as they bent over the patient later in the operating room as he lay on the table there, a gentle snore coming from his parted lips. 'Not to mention an anaesthetist.'

'Mmm,' Signy agreed, as she swabbed a neck wound, a jagged tear, with sterile gauze.

Both she and Dan were scrubbed for the case, while one of the full-time nurses at the hospital was the other registered nurse in the room—the circulating nurse. It was a small room, currently quiet and relatively peaceful after the initial rush of getting the frightened and dehydrated patient onto the operating table, an intravenous line put in to give him fluid and a painkilling drug, the wounds cleaned. Fortunately for the two men, help and first aid had come fairly quickly, as there had been other people in the area of the attack. Max, assisted by Connie, was operating on the other man.

Because the only two anaesthetists in the hospital were already engaged in other operations, their patient had to have the intravenous sedation, plus local anaesthetic injected into each wound, rather than a general anaesthetic, which was preferable. It was very time-consuming as Dan had to inject each wound several times before he could clean and stitch it without the young man feeling any pain in the deeper tissues, which would, no doubt, jerk him awake. They had been there, cleaning and stitching, for twenty minutes. It would be a long time before they finished this painstaking task. There were lacerations and bite marks on the face, neck and shoulders.

'Cougars go for the back of the neck when they attack,' Dan said softly, so that their patient, heavily sedated as he was, wouldn't hear. 'That's how they attack animals. They jump, throwing their full weight onto the intended victim's shoulders to knock him down. Hence the pattern we see before us.'

'It's…incredible,' Signy whispered. The man, in his mid-twenties, whose name was Clark Jakes, wouldn't be disfigured, but would have scars on his neck and a few on his face. 'It's a miraculous escape. This claw mark just missed the carotid artery.' She referred to the long gash in the neck that Dan was carefully suturing. They had very carefully cleaned and irrigated each wound to prevent infection.

'Yeah,' he agreed. 'A fraction of an inch deeper and he would have been a goner, I suspect.'

Dan didn't sound very English then, Signy thought inconsequentially as she shuddered mentally. Although not able to conjure up an adequate picture of a large cat attacking a man, she could picture blood pumping from a major artery in the neck.

'A good thing there were two guys together, and not just one,' he said matter-of-factly. 'That cougar will be hunted down. There's always the possibility that it has rabies, so we have to treat for that.'

Signy cut the end of the fine black silk thread that he was using to suture, noting that he was making a good job of neatening up the jagged wound, which he had first trimmed with very sharp surgical scissors. As though tuning in to her thoughts, he said, 'Suturing a wound like this isn't the same as sewing a nice clean cut made by a scalpel, is it? World Aid Doctors gives us plenty of practice in this.'

'Mmm,' she agreed. They were getting altogether too chummy for her liking; she would relax too much and end up liking him next, she told herself with exasperation.

No… He really wasn't the sort of man she liked. Too self-contained…or something. Too much in control of himself, maybe that was it—thoughtful and decisive though he was, which she found herself half admiring. She thought of what Connie had said about him—that he'd chosen his work over the woman with whom he'd lived. And then there was the case of Dominic, of course—dear, sweet Dominic, with the wonderful sense of humour in adversity. A sharp pang of grief hit her again, as it did at unexpected moments. If only the clock could be put back, how differently they would do certain things.

Perhaps she liked a certain vulnerability in a man. Really, she wasn't sure what she liked, hadn't analysed it too much. What she felt at the moment was that Dan wasn't very much like Simon who, she could see now with sudden clarity, had always taken what had been offered to him as though it had been his due, expecting and taking thoughtlessly all good things that were offered and freely given. It was odd how sometimes, when your mind was engaged on other things, you had a revelation about a particular thing that you weren't really aware had been on your mind.

She hadn't listened too attentively at the time when Connie had been telling her and the others nurses in her hut about Dan. Now she could imagine him giving all of himself to something he believed in. He was very professional, totally focussed. Once in a while she caught a brief glimpse of the English boy he must have been. Then the vision closed over and she saw a hard-headed professional who, for all his compassionate side, would clearly not allow himself to be in a position to make a mistake. Gradually, a picture was emerging. What picture was he getting of her? she wondered.

As a newcomer to this part of the world she was at a distinct disadvantage, her knowledge of the terrain and wildlife minimal. But, then, that was the situation for them when they went to a disaster zone in the course of their work—they had a very short time in which to read about the place they were going to, then it was a question of adapting quickly. It was all part of the training and the job. Nonetheless, she wished that for once the shoe was on the other foot.

Signy wondered why she was focussing so much on Dan. It must be because he was the first person she had met in the organization when she'd arrived here. She'd been thrown into his company, and he had a link with Dominic.

'We'll put a pressure dressing on that for the time being,' he said, breaking into her thoughts, 'while we get onto the next bit.'

'I have one ready here,' she said, placing a thick pad of gauze and cotton wool over the part they had sutured to prevent oozing of blood, although most of the small bleeding vessels had been tied off with catgut or coagulated with a cautery.

When they had applied the final dressings, Clark Jakes opened his eyes and mumbled something. Signy stripped off her soiled latex gloves and took his hand in hers. 'The operation's finished, Mr Jakes,' she said reassuringly, squeezing his hand. 'Everything's all right.'

'Where…?' he muttered, turning his glazed, unfocussed eyes on her face.

Signy kept hold of his hand, recalling the words that a patient had said to her once when she'd been a student nurse: 'Your hand was like a lifeline to me, Nurse, when I was very, very frightened.' Yes, she could imagine how that warm, human contact could mean so much when you were alone to face a fear, especially before and after an operation.

'You're still in the operating room in Brookes Landing Hospital, Mr Jakes,' she said, speaking slowly. 'We're going to take you out now. Squeeze my hand.'

He responded with a hard squeeze. 'That's good,' she said. 'You're more awake than I thought you were. We're going to move you onto a stretcher now.'

'His family's waiting in the ICU waiting room,' Dan said. 'I have to go up to speak to them.'

'I can imagine what they must be feeling,' Signy murmured, understanding only too well the feeling of sick fear that was experienced when someone you cared about was involved in an accident or was seriously ill. All other considerations became meaningless.

By the time the patient had been wheeled on a stretcher to a recovery area and they themselves were back in the OR, Signy felt exhausted, running on adrenalin. 'What I could use now,' she said to the other nurse, 'is a good cup of tea, followed by a litre of orange juice.'

'Maybe we can oblige with that.' The nurse laughed.

'We'll have to see about getting you and Connie a room here for the night,' Dan said, divesting himself of his soiled surgical gown, having taken time to write up a record of the surgical procedure in the patient's chart. 'There are usually a few rooms for medical staff and nurses who have to be on call or otherwise stay.'

'Don't count on it,' the nurse said. 'We've put up a lot of family members just lately for sick kids.'

'We'll see,' he said. 'We'll go back to the staff dining room by the kitchen when we've finished up here, after I've seen the family, and get something to eat.'

'That's music to my ears,' Signy said, loosening her surgical mask and letting it dangle around her neck. 'Too much has happened in too short a time.'

'Not much of a retreat for you so far,' he said, an apologetic note in his voice. He ran a hand through his untidy hair, drawing her eyes to his face, his hard, masculine mouth, the eyes serious with concentration, the nose…

'Oh, we take what comes,' she said, looking away while privately hoping that she would end this course feeling rested rather than more stressed. 'It's been… exhilarating, actually,' she added truthfully.

'Great,' he said, giving her a slightly surprised look. 'I'll see you later in the dining room, and maybe Maggie at the front desk can look into the room situation.'

'Yes…thank you,' she said. Once again, when he had gone out of the room she felt oddly relieved, as though she could now relax. She didn't know why.

'Give me a hand to clear up this room,' the nurse said, 'then we'll go in search of that cup of tea. Shouldn't take long. There's nothing else booked for this room.'

'That sounds wonderful.'

'Isn't he a QT?' The nurse, who had introduced herself as Sal, grinned at Signy as she jerked her head at the door through which Dan had departed.

'Um…QT?' Signy said, as she started to clear up the room, putting her used instruments together in a bowl, dismantling her equipment.

'Cutie,' Sal said.

'I wouldn't exactly call him that.' Signy laughed. 'Although I don't really know him, of course.'

'Oh, a lot of the girls are after him,' Sal said knowingly,

deftly bagging laundry. 'But after his split with Marianne Crowley he hasn't really looked at anyone else. She must have been off her rocker to let him slip through her fingers.'

'Don't know her,' Signy said with a shrug. 'I've just been here a very short while.'

'I don't like her,' Sal said confidentially, as though Signy had been around there for years. 'Too pushy. One of those bossy types who thinks the sun rises and sets on them. You know, very focussed on the self.'

Again they chuckled together. 'I've known a few of those,' Signy agreed.

'Sure you have,' Sal said. 'They're a world-wide breed. They have an ''I'' or a ''me'' in every sentence. Always looking out for number one.'

'If she's so awful, why would he have been interested in her?' Signy asked reasonably.

'She set out to get him,' Sal said emphatically. 'She's an attractive woman, and in a place like this a man may not meet too many women he could really go for. He's not immune. But in the case of Dan Blake she slipped up.'

'Think so?'

'Know so.'

When the two of them entered the dining room later, Connie was already there, ensconced at a table, sipping tea, a sublime, far-away look on her face.

'Ah…' She spotted Signy and waved. 'How're you doing? Weren't those cases something else? Those poor guys, eh? They'll have nightmares, I guess, for a long time to come. I can imagine it—scared to go out in the sticks on your own or without a shotgun.'

'Yes,' Signy said feelingly. 'I can hardly believe it—it seems sort of unreal to me.'

'Well, it would. You'd better believe it,' Connie said. 'This is Sal.'

'Hi.'

The tea was wonderful, drunk between mouthfuls of sustaining sandwiches.

Dan came into the room with Max. Moments later, two other doctors, identifiable by their white lab coats, followed them in. One was a woman, strikingly attractive, with thick, curly black hair tied behind with a ribbon. The hair contrasted dramatically with a pale, creamy skin, and her eyes were dark also.

'That's her,' Sal hissed, nudging Signy's arm so that the cup of tea she was holding slopped some of its contents onto the table. They felt as though they really had known each other for years, having had a baptism of fire, so to speak. 'That's the Marianne Crowley I was talking to you about.'

'I didn't suppose there was more than one of them,' Signy said sardonically.

'Eh? Oh, you English! I wouldn't be surprised if she's regretting giving up on him. Look at her!' Sal said, frankly staring, while Connie caught Signy's eye and grinned slightly, raising her glance heavenward. So this was small-town intrigue, her glance said.

'Please, don't nudge me again, Sal,' Signy said, mopping up spilled tea with a paper napkin.

'Eh? Look!' Sal gripped Signy's arm, slopping more tea.

Discreetly, Signy looked towards where Dan was standing, to see the dark, dramatic-looking woman kiss him on the cheek. He kissed her back. They were smiling at each other while Max stood by.

'I'm really not interested,' Signy said, feeling an odd irritation at having to be a party to this public display of affection, as well as the gossip.

'What? You off your rocker, too?' Sal said, incredulous. 'Everyone here's interested in Dan Blake. There's a shortage of great guys, unless you want a logger—that sort of thing.'

'I don't want anyone,' Signy said tartly. 'I'm only here for four months. Anyway, he's not my type. Assuming, of course, that he would be the slightest bit interested in me.'

Sal looked at her uncomprehendingly. 'I don't think he knows I exist as a woman,' she said wistfully.

'That nose…' Signy began.

'I *love* that nose,' Sal whispered dreamily.

'What about Max?' Connie said to Sal, a subtle glint in her eye.

'He's great, too,' Sal said. 'He just hasn't got much staying power. You know, he knows he's in great demand, so he runs off in all directions, spreading himself around.'

Moments later, Terri and Pearl came into the dining room, and there was a general reunion, as though they hadn't seen each other for ages. Attention was diverted away from the small group of doctors as the nurses chatted and drank tea.

'Was someone else looking for a room?' a voice interrupted them. Maggie from Reception was standing there.

'Oh, I am,' Signy said. 'I suppose we're not going back tonight to the island?'

'No,' Terri said. 'I think I got the last room, if you can call it a room. More like a cupboard with a window. You can bunk on the floor if you have to.'

'She's right, there's no other room in the hospital. I'm sorry,' Maggie said. 'We've had a run on rooms for various reasons, and we don't have many spare to begin with. We'll think of something.'

'It's all right, Maggie,' a masculine voice interrupted, 'I'll deal with it.' Dan had come over to their table. 'She can stay with me at Heron Cottage. I've two spare rooms.'

'OK, Dr Blake,' Maggie said, retreating.

'If that's all right with you, Signy,' Dan said, fixing her with his astute gaze, his expression unreadable. He was still wearing the green scrub suit that he had worn in the operating room, which revealed arms that were muscular and tanned, in spite of his leanness.

Out of the corner of her eye Signy could see that Sal's jaw had dropped, and that an expression of open-mouthed stupefaction did not become her. Neither did the avid shifting of her eyes from face to face, from Signy to Dan and back again, as though she were watching a television soap-opera and that she herself were invisible. The continuing saga of…Signy thought. Now there should be a roll of drums or something. Perhaps this sort of thing— the romantic relationships, and rumours of relationships— grabbed the attention in a small place, perhaps to counteract the cruel drama of such things as cougar attacks. Well, count me out.

Signy cleared her throat as she looked up at Dan, feeling herself grow a little hot under the intense scrutiny of Sal, who appeared to be waiting for the next revelation. 'That's very kind of you, Dr Blake,' she said evenly. 'It looks as though I might have to take you up on that.'

'She could stay with me—' Sal had found her voice '—except that I live in cougar country when I'm not on call here, and she being English and all, that wouldn't be fair. Why, I'm even scared myself.'

'Quite,' Dan said dryly. 'There's something for you to pass around on the internal telegraph. I'll see you in the lobby, Signy, in about three-quarters of an hour, if that's all right. I still have a few things to do here.'

She nodded. 'Thanks.'

When Dan had joined his MD colleagues, the uncrushable Sal leaned forward across the table. 'I'd give my eye teeth to be in your position,' she said excitedly, unfazed by Dan's last remark.

'What position is that?' Signy queried.

'Obviously not the one she has in mind,' Connie chipped in.

Pearl and Terri were wide-eyed.

'If you need me to spell it out for you, you want your head examined,' Sal said incredulously. 'You should have seen the way that Dr Crowley was looking at him when he was talking to you. If you ask me, she still has something going for him. It was her fault that they split up, and now I get the impression that he's gone off her.'

'You must have eyes in the back of your head, then,' Connie said, 'since she's behind you.'

'I took a look.'

'Maybe he has gone off her, maybe not,' Connie said. 'It's no business of yours.'

'And what about the old West Indian saying in relation to past affairs,' Signy said, getting into the spirit of the discussion, 'which says, "It don't take much for the old fire stick to ketch back up".'

There was a second or two of silence from the other four at the table, then a burst of laughter, causing other people in the room to look at them.

'Bingo!' Connie said.

'Well,' Signy said, standing up, 'time to get out of this gear and into normal clothing. Is there any place in the OR where we can get a shower?'

'Sure,' Sal said. 'Hey, wait a minute. How will I know what happened?'

'You won't.'

'But—'

'Come on, Signy.' Connie rose to her feet also. 'Let's find that shower.'

It was great to be clean and fresh again and to have a change of clothing. They had each been asked to bring a small overnight bag for just this eventuality. Signy ran a hand through her newly washed hair, which was still damp, while she waited for Dan. Now that the excitement was over, she desperately wanted to sleep.

'Hi!' Suddenly he was there behind her, ready to leave, dressed in casual outdoor clothing, his hair also damp. He had that chronically exhausted expression that she had come to recognize so well. 'Ready?'

'Oh…um…yes,' she said hesitantly, flooded with doubt now that he was there and the two of them were alone. Negative feelings about him were coming to the fore again. The helpful Maggie had departed from her post and there was no one else about.

Seeing something amiss in her expression, he stood looking at her sardonically for a few seconds. 'Changed your mind?'

'Um, no,' she said quickly. 'I appreciate your invitation. It's very kind.'

'No, it isn't,' he said, with that wry twist to his mouth that was becoming familiar to her. 'It's expedient. Come on.'

Then they were outside in the fresh, cool air. Now that evening was approaching, the temperature had dropped. Just beyond the entrance doors Dan stopped and took her arm, detaining her. 'I'm not looking for any sort of involvement, you know. That's the last thing on my mind.'

The way he said it sounded like an insult to her. With a supreme effort she prevented herself from flushing. 'I...didn't assume you were,' she said.

'You make it only too clear what you think of me,' he said tersely. 'Perhaps you'd keep it to yourself, so that any negative vibes don't get through to my colleagues here, with whom I have to work permanently after all you temporary people have gone.'

'I...I'm sorry,' she said, taken aback by the sudden vehemence in him. 'I didn't mean...'

Dan walked on, and she followed, going towards the car that had been parked nearby. 'And as for that guy you mentioned, Dominic Fraser, I don't actually remember him personally, but I do recall, vaguely, that he did some rather stupid things, and I intend to check up on the records to find out the details,' he said, his face tense.

Signy said nothing, not wanting to get into any sort of argument, sensing that he was as exhausted as she was. In silence they got into the car. 'Please,' she said, her voice small, 'could we just forget about it for now?'

'Sure. But I intend to get to the bottom of it,' he said as he did up his seat belt with quick, decisive movements that hinted at exasperation. 'By the way, to give credit where credit is due, thank you for your help with that case. I wouldn't have wanted to do it without a scrub nurse.'

His sudden change of tack left her nonplussed. 'I'm glad I could be of help. I didn't really have a choice, did I? So it wasn't as though I was doing you a favour.'

'Like me offering you a room,' he said. 'Now we're even, I guess. So you can quit patronizing me.'

'Patronizing?' she said, incredulous and angry. 'I wouldn't know how to be patronizing.'

⁎ To that, he said nothing. They drove in silence the short distance to the small wooden house, Heron Cottage, that was really no more than a pretty, sturdy shack with an attic. Stiffly Signy got out and, without looking directly at him, followed him to the door.

'I'll show you around,' he said when they were inside, his voice tight and controlled. 'You can get yourself something to eat when you feel like it—there's plenty of food in the kitchen. I have to go out again to do a few things. The guest room is on the ground floor, with its own bathroom, over here. You do whatever you like— sleep, or whatever.'

Signy nodded dumbly, not trusting her voice as he showed her the small, sparsely furnished room that was cosy and comfortable at the same time. At that moment she felt like crying, a complete contrast to the mood of hilarity she had shared with the other nurses in the staff dining room.

'I'll show you the kitchen,' Dan said.

Apart from the guest bedroom, the kitchen and a small study, the ground floor was taken up with a large sitting room that had a huge open fireplace piled with logs waiting to be set alight, kindling and crumpled newspapers around them. Her eyes lingered on the fireplace, as she thought how nice it would be to sit by such a log fire now that the temperature had dropped. Side stairs led up to the upper level, where Dan must have his room, she thought.

Dan opened cupboard doors in the kitchen, then the door of a very large refrigerator. 'Help yourself to anything here,' he said.

Again she nodded, thanking him in a voice that was

barely audible, wondering if he would accuse her of being patronizing again by her thanks.

When they were out in the sitting room again and he was preparing to take his leave, she found the courage to say what was on her mind. 'You know, Dr Blake, you don't have to have me here if you would rather not. I can quite easily share a room with Terri Carpenter. She offered.'

Tiredly he looked at her, his eyes narrowing as an expression almost of hauteur crossed his face. 'I don't think you would want to sleep on the floor…and I wouldn't want you to do that. Make yourself comfortable. Better not go outside—there's a fair amount of wildlife out here after dark. I expect I'll see you later.'

'Wait! What have I done to make you so…irritable with me?' she blurted out.

'I don't like being made the butt of gossip,' he said. 'Most of the time I take it in my stride, but once in a while I get a little sick of it.'

'But that wasn't me,' she said. 'I don't know anything about you.' At the time she hadn't considered that he might have heard something of Sal's confidences. Tact wasn't something the other nurse possessed in any great measure, it seemed. What she, Signy, did know about Dan, she corrected herself mentally, had nothing to do with his love life.

He looked at her consideringly, then shrugged. Then he was gone, the door locking itself behind him, leaving her standing in the sitting room, surrounded by comfortable chairs and two long sofas.

When he had driven away, Signy was left in complete silence. Not even a clock ticked in the house. There was no sound of wind, or any other sound of nature, or of man. Slowly she went into the bedroom and shut the door.

Having had tea at the hospital, she wasn't hungry. Perhaps later she would cook something.

She eased off her shoes, took off her outer clothing and got into the bed, turning her face to the wall. What she needed now was sleep, more than anything else, she told herself. First and foremost, you had to look after yourself, otherwise you wouldn't be any good to anyone and could be a liability. That much she had learned from the job she was doing. Images of the man mauled by the cougar were imposed on her inner vision. She still felt like crying, and as she lay there with eyes closed, tears began to seep from beneath her lids and run down her cheeks.

Dominic was coming towards her in brilliant sunlight, his eyes squinting against it; he was wearing the Australian bush hat that he liked, the khaki shirt with the sleeves rolled up to the elbows, the long cotton trousers. Behind him was the dried brown grass of the plain, reaching into the distance, the few stunted trees.

'Dom! Dom!' Her lips framed his name as she watched him approaching. He seemed to be taking a long time to get to her.

Then she was on the motorbike, the ramshackle vehicle that had seen better days, which miraculously kept on going, bumping and bouncing over rough tracks that had never been intended for anything as civilized as a motorized vehicle. It was her hands that were on the handlebars, controlling the machine with effort, wet with sweat on the rubber grips. The whole thing was low to the ground with her weight and that of the injured man behind her, his leg with the bloody bandage held stiffly at the side as they bounced and swayed sickeningly.

She could see the brown-red rust on the handlebars, the vegetation on the path dried up from lack of water, could feel the sun burning through the burnoose and turban that she had over her head and shoulders, half covering her face below the tinted goggles that she wore, could feel the heat on her shoulders and back that she had protected with layers of cotton.

Then the machine was tipping to one side as they hit a stone and she was struggling to prevent it from falling over, wrestling with it as though it were a live thing, instinctively trying to stop it from tipping over onto the side where the man, her rescuer, had the injured leg. That would have been no way to repay him. Close to the ground as they were, she slowed and flung out an arm and a leg to stop the fall. There was a crash, the sound of breaking…

Signy sat up in bed. A faint light from somewhere outside penetrated the darkness of the room, and there was a sound of wind in tree branches. In her head was the African sunlight, harsh and burning; here was a velvety darkness, closing around her like a cloak, a coolness.

Beside the bed on the floor was the lamp that had been on a table at her side. The shade had come away from the base, while the ceramic base lay broken beside it, neatly split into several large pieces which showed white in the half-light.

She swung her legs over the edge of the bed, knelt down on the floor and picked up the pieces, holding them gently in her hands. They looked like pieces of the moon fallen to the ground. Vaguely she recalled the lamp, intact, on the table. Superimposed on that image was the face of Dominic.

A light clicked on in the room but she didn't look up. On her bare thighs her hands rested, limp, holding the broken pieces. An inertia had come over her. Warm tears dropped from her eyes. She supposed they came from her; she didn't know, because she felt distanced from what was around her, as though her mind were split in two, part of it a long way away, with people and places that no longer existed as she had known them. Where the makeshift medical station had stood there would now be only charred remains, blowing away in the relentless hot wind, the people she had known long gone. For a long time, it seemed, she knelt, hunched over as though in prayer.

'Signy,' a voice said, and at last she looked up.

Dan stood in the doorway of her room, looking at her. She saw that he wore a dressing-gown, that his feet were bare, that his hair was untidy from sleep, that his tired, angular face showed concern. Slowly, dazedly, her eyes moved over him. The twisted nose gave his face a some-how reassuring familiarity, and she sighed involuntarily.

It came back to her then by slow increments that she was a guest in his house, that she had somehow broken his lamp, that she had just experienced one of the vivid dreams, in brilliant colour and in great detail, that had haunted her for months since she had left Africa. It was a healing process, she believed, a way for the mind to sort out during sleep the happenings that at the time had come too fast and furiously to fully comprehend…nature's way of helping one make sense of them, if there was any sense to be made.

There was no point in trying to stop the tears—they would stop of their own accord, eventually.

'Signy,' he said again softly, still standing there.

Then she became aware that she was almost naked, that she'd slept from the time she'd got into bed late the previous afternoon, that she hadn't risen again to cook herself supper or put on the nightclothes she'd brought with her. When she looked down at herself she saw the black silk bra that had small yellow roses printed on it, the edging of her panties having the same pattern. Like a scene in a tableau, she knelt there, vulnerable, holding the broken lamp as though in supplication, her shoulders hunched.

'I've somehow broken your lamp,' she whispered. 'I'm sorry.'

He came over to her, knelt down and took the broken pieces from her carefully and placed them under the bed, his quick movements creating a cool breeze around her so that Signy became intensely aware that she wasn't clothed and the room was cold.

'It doesn't matter,' he said. 'Get up.'

Obediently she stood up, letting him put a robe on her which he'd taken from a hanger behind the door. As she stood there inertly, he tied the belt for her. 'Come on. Careful where you tread, there might be some slivers of lamp,' he said, taking her hand and leading her to one of the big sofas that dominated the sitting room. 'Lie down there.' He moved a cushion so that she could put her head on it, so that she lay facing the fireplace.

Moments later Dan came back with a pillow and the duvet from her bed. Mutely she received his ministrations, finding comfort from a rare sense of being cared for as he covered her up. Again she was conscious of being a long way from home. Her face was still wet with tears and she was shivering.

'Don't move from there,' he said. The tight look of irritation that had been on his face when he'd left the house in the afternoon had gone, replaced by a serious, almost professional scrutiny. That expression softened when their eyes met and he knelt down beside her. 'All right?'

Signy nodded. The familiar feeling of sadness that had been with her when she'd woken up lifted a little when they looked at each other. Unconvinced, his eyes roved over her features, willing her to talk to him, she knew, but not compelling her. Their faces were very close, and she found herself returning his scrutiny unselfconsciously, as though she were an observer of the scene, watching herself looking at him. That other self, coolly removed, focussed on his hard mouth and wanted to lean forward to kiss him, wondering whether she would actually do so. Something told her that he regretted the brusqueness he'd shown her when they'd last spoken.

Her eyes followed him as he went into the kitchen. She listened to him running water into a kettle, moving about. Often when she had one of those dreams there was no one else there. Sometimes she wrote her dreams down in a notebook, trying to wrest meaning from them. It also gave her something concrete to do afterwards, a sense of being in control.

When Dan came back he was carrying two glasses of clear brownish liquid. 'Drink that, Signy,' he said, offering her one. 'It's brandy in warm water with a bit of honey. It'll help you to relax.'

'Thank you.' Again she wanted to say she was sorry—for waking him up when he so clearly needed sleep and for putting him to trouble—but she held her peace. From his matter-of-fact accepting demeanor she understood instinctively that he knew all about nightmares.

After taking a swallow of his own drink, he went over to the vast fireplace and lifted off a few of the logs, then lit the paper under the ones that remained. Signy watched him, still not fully in the here-and-now mentally. The paper and kindling flared up, filling the room with flickering light and a sweet smell of wood smoke, a reassuring, primal scent. When it was burning well he walked over to the windows and drew the curtains, shutting out the darkness, while still she watched him. The room became cosy, a safe, enclosed world.

Next, he moved a small table and pushed the other sofa parallel to the one she was lying on so that it was close to hers, about six inches away. As Signy sipped the warm, comforting drink, she understood that he intended them to sleep there, that he would be with her, and her tears seemed to fall faster, tears of gratitude. That feeling, together with her antipathy towards him, created such a feeling of dissonance that she felt despair and confusion imposing itself on the comfort she was deriving from his presence.

'Drink up,' he said, looking sideways at her as he tended to the fire, his face half-hidden in the shadows. 'You'll feel better afterwards.'

The drink was good, just enough honey in it to take the bitterness away from the brandy. He didn't ask her about her dream, and she sensed that he wasn't going to do so. In her own good time she would talk…or not.

The brandy induced a warm glow in her, seeming to reflect the outward glow of the crackling log fire. Gradually Signy felt herself coming back to this new reality of being in another country, far removed from the events of her dreams. Having to sleep on a sofa, a few inches away from her new colleague, seemed just part and parcel of the type of life that they had elected to undertake. This mutual support helped them to keep going. Wasn't that what she had done with Dominic? Sometimes there was a fine line between helping and being foolhardy. Somehow she would work through it all and the dreams would become less frequent.

When the drinks were finished, Dan squeezed past her to get onto the other sofa to lie down under his own duvet. 'Snuggle down, Signy. Make yourself comfortable,' he instructed her. She had been watching his every move, propped up on one elbow, like one passively watching a film, gaining comfort from familiar motions, blotting out her dream, so now she lay back against the pillow.

Unexpectedly, as she lay on her back, looking up at the flickering firelight, he leaned across to her, his face close to hers. 'Tomorrow's going to be a busy day for both of us,' he said. 'Try to concentrate on that. I have more visits to make, a clinic to run at the hospital in the afternoon. I want you to help me, and I think you should stay here for one more night.'

He leaned forward and kissed her gently on the cheek. 'Try to sleep now,' he said.

When he was comfortable in his own bed, she felt his hand touch her arm. 'Give me your hand,' he said.

Across that small divide he held her hand, his grasp dry, warm and firm.

The last thing she remembered before falling asleep was the comforting feel of a warm hand holding hers. The first thing she was aware of when she awoke was muted daylight shining into her eyes, then the smell of freshly made coffee.

Signy was lying on her side on the sofa, facing the other one which had been Dan's bed, now empty, with the bed-clothes in disarray. She had slept heavily and dreamlessly for the remainder of the night. Easing herself over onto her back, she reviewed the events of the night, the vividness of the earlier dream.

'Good morning. Coffee?' Dan's voice broke into her obsessive thoughts.

'Oh…yes.' Signy raised her head to look at Dan standing in the doorway of the kitchen. 'Please. It smells good. Just what I need. I'll get up. I've no idea what time it is.'

She was still wearing the robe that he'd given her the night before.

'No, stay there. I'll bring it to you. It's early yet,' he said.

'Thanks.' Signy ran a hand through her untidy hair, then got up to go to the bathroom, feeling self-conscious in the robe with this man who was little more than a stranger. However, this was no time for false modesty.

When she got back he had shifted the furniture to its original position, and there was a tray of coffee things on the low table, plus a plate of croissants that gave off a fresh aroma and a pot of honey. There were several things that she wanted to say to him—an apology for disturbing him in the night, for one—yet she kept silent, sensing that he didn't want her to keep saying she was sorry all the time.

'Help yourself,' he said, sitting down opposite her and pouring himself coffee from a pot. To her he seemed overtly masculine, rumpled from sleep, hair untidy, a growth of stubble on his face. Surreptitiously, she looked at him, feeling a reluctant womanly interest in him that left her angry at herself, falling into the mode that Sal appeared to be in. Immediately she strove to dismiss such fledgling feelings. He was the enemy, until she or he could prove otherwise.

'Just what I needed,' she said appreciatively, yet feeling the artificiality of the polite verbal exchanges when her thoughts and emotions were churning. There was a certain tension of things left unsaid, as well as from a mutual determination not to disrupt the spurious equilibrium that existed between them for now. 'You make a very good cup of coffee.' Although she was sitting back comfortably, she didn't feel exactly comfortable.

When she glanced at him, there was a slight hint of

amusement again on his face, a warmth in his eyes. He inclined his head. 'Thank you,' he said.

'Is something about me amusing you, Dr Blake?' she said.

'Don't take this the wrong way…you look very cute in a man's dressing gown,' he said, looking at her assessingly. 'And you don't have to revert to calling me Dr Blake, Signy.'

You don't look too bad yourself, she wanted to say, but didn't. And she wondered what he'd thought of her black silk bra with the yellow roses, which was rather pretty. The memory of it made her flush, and she sensed that he was thinking about it too, how she had knelt on the floor with the broken lamp in her hands. 'You were rather irritable with me yesterday,' she said, 'so I think that a certain formality might be better.'

'I'm sorry for that. Forget it.'

'I can't forget it, and you can't expect me to pretend that it wasn't that way,' she countered.

'Forgive me, then,' he said.

Signy shrugged. 'I'll see,' she said. 'May I ask what the precise plans are for today?' She forced a casualness and a retreat to a safer topic.

'First, I want to visit our patient who was attacked by the cougar. I want to make sure the wounds aren't getting infected. He's on IV antibiotics. I called the hospital very early this morning and he's all right so far. Then I have a few more house calls to make of a general nature, then an obstetrics clinic for prenatal and postnatal patients at the hospital. There are quite a lot of women giving birth around here.'

'A busy day,' she said automatically, her thoughts going over what they would have to do.

'Dr Marianne Crowley, who does general medicine,

also sees some of those patients when I'm not around, although she prefers not to do deliveries. Of course, she can't do Caesarean sections, she's not a surgeon. She works up here for part of the year.'

Signy nodded. 'I see,' she said, careful not to react in any way at the mention of the woman who had once meant something to him, and maybe still did. She didn't want to put herself in the category of gossip, with the avid Sal.

The dawn light was slowly changing from pale grey to pale yellow. Still they sat opposite each other, drinking a second mug of coffee.

'In this job,' she said, as though compelled to speak by his quiet air of waiting, his will overcoming hers perhaps, 'you lose your innocence. You lose your faith that things will turn out all right.' Signy didn't look at him, keeping her eyes on the mug that she held in her hands on her lap. 'It frightens me sometimes.'

'And your dream?' he said gently.

Haltingly, she told him about her dream, still not looking at him.

'Who was the man on the motorbike?' he said.

'He came from the organization to rescue me—from the head camp. He was a South African named Joachim...very brave, very sensible. If it hadn't been for him I might not be here, talking about it. I'm beginning to realize that now.'

'Go on,' he said.

'On the way to get to me he had an accident with the bike and injured his knee, but managed to get back on and drive to me. I was the only one left behind at the medical station, you see. I wanted to wait for Dominic because he'd gone to look for some UN people. All the others had gone already. I had to drive the bike out, with

Joachim on the back…he was in a lot of pain. I put a dressing on the knee and splinted it.'

Again Dan waited.

'In retrospect, of course, it seems madness that I stayed behind, now I know that the medical station was subsequently burnt out by rebels, whoever they were. But at the time it seemed all right to me, even though I wasn't sure how I was going to get out. The others had said they would send someone back for me…and Dominic. I…had such a naïve faith that we would get out, both of us.' Signy's voice trailed off.

'Only Dominic didn't show,' Dan prompted softly, matter-of-factly, 'by the time you really had to leave?'

'No…' she whispered. 'The system failed him.'

CHAPTER FIVE

'THE pace is pretty slow, isn't it?' Terri said, *sotto voce*, to Signy as they stood in the obstetrics clinic that afternoon, waiting for their next patient to arrive for her appointment. 'You know, at this rate, Signy, we might lose our survival skills.' She giggled slightly. 'Not that I'm complaining, mind you. I could do with a little break, especially after yesterday, seeing those two guys who'd been mauled by the cougar.'

'Yes, don't knock it, Terri,' Signy said, sitting down behind the reception desk. The nurse who worked there regularly had gone off to the dining room for a teabreak, leaving the two World Aid nurses to hold the fort for half an hour or so. Dan was behind the scenes somewhere, writing up charts from the patients he'd seen already. Their next patient was late.

Signy knew exactly what Terri meant about losing survival skills. In the work they did, the places they went to, they had to hone their instincts to assess situations constantly. Sometimes they got it wrong, she knew that.

That morning she and Terri had made some more home visits with Dan, while Connie and Pearl had gone with Max to do the same, and now the other two nurses were in the emergency department. The other nurses in the group who had been on Kelp Island had gone to other parts of the mainland with other doctors.

'Dan asked us this morning if we wanted to stay in Brookes Landing until Friday,' Terri said, 'then go back to the island so that we can have a long weekend off to rest. After all, we are supposed to be resting some of the time. I said it was all right with me to stay here—it makes more sense than going back and forth, even though it is only about twenty minutes by plane. What do you think, Signy? You're the one who's sharing his cottage.'

That morning Signy had told Terri about her bad dream. 'Oh, I get them all the time,' Terri had said. 'For quite a while I was scared to go to sleep, but they're getting fewer.'

'It does make sense to stay here,' Signy agreed. 'It was a bit odd being in the same house with him because he was bad-tempered yesterday, but he was very sweet to me when I needed someone.'

Terri looked at her consideringly. 'I think he's basically a very nice guy,' she said. 'Men get huffy like that when they're attracted to a woman and don't want to admit it to themselves, because it's inconvenient, let alone admit it to anyone else or the woman involved.'

'I don't think there's anything like that,' Signy said. 'Actually, although he's nice to me when he has to be, I think he really thinks I'm pretty naïve, and is barely hiding the fact that he's impatient with me. I get the impression that he doesn't think I'm cut out to be in World Aid Nurses.'

'Mmm. Who is, really?' Terri said. 'Is there a type? To have common sense, be calm in a crisis... I think those things count for a lot, and I would say that you have those qualities as much as anyone else here. There are people who are very intelligent but don't have any common sense, we've all met those.'

Signy laughed. 'Yes, I've met a few.'

'Dan's spent an awful lot of time with you,' Terri went on, 'and he could have left you to share a room with one of us.'

'You're getting like Sal.' Signy grinned.

'Heaven forbid!'

'He spends time with me because he's watching me, Terri. That's what I think, anyway.' As she said that, a conviction of its veracity grew into a certainty. 'And that's not a compliment. He's waiting to pounce, I suspect, to pick up on something negative, waiting for me to slip up so that he can report back to headquarters that I'm not the type they're looking for.'

'A bit late for that. What makes you think that, anyway?' Terri asked.

'He asked me a lot of questions when we were driving into the camp, like whether I could drive a motorboat or ski, as though they were essential requirements.'

'Huh! Don't let it worry you. I don't suppose he's really in a great position to judge you, Signy. Maybe he just wants to help, knowing we've all been traumatized by our experiences. Max is always asking me if I want to unburden myself to him,' Terri said.

'Did you?'

'No. I didn't feel ready, and I'm not sure he's the right person. I guess I'll know when I'm ready.'

'Mmm,' Signy murmured in agreement.

'Have you seen anything of Sal, by the way?'

'No. She'll be quizzing me, no doubt. '

'I hope I never get like that,' Terri said, 'where my whole life revolves around a tiny place and its gossip. Maybe that's why we're with World Aid Nurses to begin with.'

'Yes, you have something there. I try to analyse why I'm doing what I'm doing, why I'm here...and I can't come up with a good answer, except I feel that it's right. Even so, sometimes I think I must be mad.'

'I know what you mean. There are no half-measures in what we do, are there? You're either in or you're out.'

The telephone on the desk shrilled. 'Obstetrics clinic,' Signy said into the receiver.

'Is Dr Blake there, please? This is the labour room, I'm one of the nurses here,' a voice informed her. 'We need him up here right away to look at one of his patients in labour. She's not progressing, and I think a Caesarean section might be in order.'

'He's here,' Signy said. 'I'll get him for you.'

Dan, wearing a white lab coat over a green scrub suit, was sitting at a desk in a tiny office behind the scenes, hunched over a pile of patents' charts. 'A phone call for you, Dr Blake,' she said, going on to explain the reason for the call.

Dan stood up, stretched and ran a hand through his already ruffled hair. 'I thought I might have to do a C-section on that woman,' he said. 'Would you like to come up there with me, then help me in the operating room if need be? I shall have a scrub nurse but not an assistant surgeon, which is what you would have to be.'

Immediately she wanted to ask him if he was inviting her so that he could watch her, but bit back the retort, telling herself not to be paranoid.

'Yes,' she agreed, 'I would like to do that.' Since theatre work was her specialty, she knew that he would have no reason to find fault with her. Don't get paranoid, she admonished herself again. That was the last thing she needed, on top of the guilt of being alive while Dominic was dead, as well as having the dreams to contend with.

Even so, as she followed him out to the reception area, she found herself agreeing with Terri that he did arrange things so that she was spending an inordinate amount of time with him, and again the sense was growing that she couldn't put a flattering connotation on that.

'We'll go up to the labour room first while I take another look at my patient. Come up to the OR with us, Terri,' Dan was saying. 'It looks as though we have a C-section to do, and you may as well help the circulating nurse and see how things are done in a very small community hospital, especially as I know you come from a high-powered teaching hospital.'

'Thanks,' Terri said. 'I'd like to. The clinic nurse just came back, so I'm ready.'

'I'll tell her where we're going. My other patients will have to wait,' Dan said. 'Tomorrow you two should spend time in the emergency department, to see what types of accidents we get here, coming in from the backwoods and from the sea.'

In the operating rooms Signy and Terri changed into blue scrub suits, then walked down a short corridor to the designated room where the operation would take place, Dan having decided that they needed to operate right away. Just as Dan came out of the room to meet them at the scrub sinks, Max came out of a room opposite.

'Ah!' Max exclaimed with exaggerated delight, coming over to Signy and Terri and putting his arms round their shoulders. In his green scrub suit he looked every bit the part of the dashing surgeon. 'I do love having you girls here. You bring a breath of fresh air to this backwater.'

Terri grinned, lapping it up, though evidently taking Max with a pinch of salt, while Signy found his company relaxing after the odd tension of being with Dan, the apparent complexity of his character. Max was more of a type, or so she thought, and therefore more manageable.

Dan viewed this little scene with a wryness that was almost comic, and Signy suppressed a grin. Getting along well with all and sundry was part of the job, a skill that one had to learn, sometimes painfully, sometimes only understanding in retrospect what one had learnt.

'Go to it, girls!' Max said, waving them goodbye as he strode, in all his masculine splendour, down the corridor.

'Saving lives and fighting disease,' Terri commented as they watched him go, not caring that Dan was there. 'Wow! He's cute, but if there's one thing nurses hate it's being referred to as girls.'

'Here, *girls*,' Dan said, grinning at them, 'come in here to the scrub sinks and get suited up.'

In a small anteroom they all donned caps and masks. 'Get yourself in there, Terri,' he went on, 'and help the circulating nurse, her name's Patty. The patient's already on the operating table. Her name's Mrs Weaver—she prefers that to being addressed by her first name. The anaesthetist's there, ready to go. We're going to give her a general anaesthetic. We'll prep the operating site before he puts her under. Signy, you get scrubbed here with me.'

When they were alone, Signy began the scrub process.

'There's something you said to me this morning, Signy,' Dan said quietly, standing next to her as he tore open a pack containing a sterile scrub brush, 'that I've been thinking about. You said that the system failed Dominic Fraser. I made some enquiries by phone today to the headquarters in Vancouver. The system didn't fail him, Signy. He failed himself. It may seem unkind, and perhaps irrelevant, to say that now, but sadly it's the truth.'

'I…don't think this is the time to talk about it, Dr Blake,' she said, while she felt as though her heart were contracting, as once again the image of Dominic as she had seen him in her dream, and so many times in real life, with the bush hat on, squinting into the African sun, came vividly to her. He had always been so full of life and a sense of adventure, revelling in the fact that he was on the continent where he had always dreamed of being. That energy and promise were gone for ever. It was unbearable. Signy found her agitation growing.

'Maybe,' Dan said quietly, soaping his arms. 'I've been wanting to say it, and I couldn't hold off any longer. Just think about the fact that he put you in danger as well. Not that you were a passive victim. We'll talk about it some other time.'

'He didn't know I was going to hang around there,' she said hotly, 'at the medical station, waiting for him.' By saying that, she had condemned herself out of her own mouth. 'He had no way of knowing.'

Dan merely looked at her sideways as he washed his arms, the expression telling her that he understood what had happened and why, that he had expected as much. 'We'll put it aside for now,' he said.

The thought came to her strongly that he'd said those things just before they were to do an operation, with her as the surgical assistant, in order to put her off her stride, to test her, to see how she shaped up under stress. Then she dismissed the idea immediately as being paranoid. Instead of the ready angry retort that was on the tip of her tongue, she bit her lip hard and bent her head to the task of scrubbing her hands and arms under the warm running water. The presence of Dan at the sink next to her, his arm a few inches away from hers, made her feel on edge, compounding the agitation she already felt.

Their patient, thirty-nine years old and having her first baby, had been somewhat distressed when they'd seen her in the labour unit. She had been told that the labour wasn't progressing and that she had a large baby that was in the breech position. As Signy went into the operating room to put on a sterile gown and gloves, she saw that Mrs Weaver was calmer now that things were in progress, so she went over to her to give a few words of encouragement.

Electronic monitors recorded the vital signs of blood pressure, pulse rate, respiration, temperature and circulating oxygen. Signy took all this in at a glance as she shrugged into her gown, seeing also a foetal monitor in place which told them the vital signs of the baby inside the uterus.

'We're going to clean your skin and put some sterile drapes on you first, Mrs Weaver,' Dan explained to her, as a nurse tied up his sterile gown at the back. 'Then, when we're absolutely ready to start, we'll give you the anaesthetic.'

Their patient, who had an oxygen mask over her nose and mouth as she lay flat on the operating table, could only nod slightly in understanding. Still in active labour, she groaned about every two minutes as a strong contraction hit her. Although the staff needed to hurry to make a start and to get the baby delivered as soon as possible, they went about their task very calmly and methodically.

'This will be a little cold on the skin,' Dan said, as the scrub nurse handed him a small container of iodine prep solution and a gauze sponge on a long metal holder. With long, even strokes, he swiftly cleaned the woman's protuberant abdomen, then he and Signy draped her with large blue sterile drapes so that only a small portion of her abdomen was visible, the part where they would make the incision. All the while, the doctor who was to give the anaesthetic talked quietly to the woman, bending down close to her, letting her know what was happening.

When the instrument tables were in place and the staff in their positions to start the operation—with Signy, as the assistant surgeon, on the opposite side of the table from Dan—he nodded at the anaesthetist. 'Ready,' he said quietly.

From now, things would move quickly. While feeling a little nervous, as if she was somehow on trial, Signy had to admire Dan's way of doing things so far. She did it grudgingly. His calm professionalism, his empathy with the patient, couldn't be faulted. She took a deep breath and let it out slowly, willing herself to be calm.

As the anaesthetist injected the drugs into the patient's IV line that would put her to sleep, then intubated her and connected up the tubing to the anaesthetic machine, Signy armed herself with a large gauze sponge with which to soak up blood. The scrub nurse silently handed Dan a scalpel. Then the anaesthetist looked up from his expertly executed task and nodded.

Dan quickly and smoothly used the scalpel to make a long horizontal incision through the skin at the lower end of the abdomen. Signy, letting out a pent-up breath on a quiet sigh, pressed her gauze sponge against the multiple small beads of blood that appeared instantly along the line of the incision.

The baby, a large boy weighing just over eleven pounds, was alive and apparently well.

'Wow!' the scrub nurse and the circulating nurse said in unison as Dan eased the oversized baby by the feet through the incision he had made. As he did so, Signy quickly suctioned up amniotic fluid and blood that flowed out of the uterus at the same time.

Holding the baby firmly by his ankles, with the other hand supporting his back, Dan put him down quickly and carefully into the baby resuscitation cart nearby so that the paediatrician, who was ready and waiting, could attend to him by sucking mucus from his throat and stimulating him to breathe.

'Wow!' Signy echoed softly, glancing briefly at the baby before she and Dan attended to the task at hand, which was to deliver the placenta from the uterus, prevent any unnecessary bleeding and to stop existing bleeding as much as possible. Then they had to sew up the incision in the uterus. Signy concentrated on suctioning and sponging.

Just then the baby gave a tentative, gurgling cry, followed by two or three seconds of silence and a stronger cry. A collective wave of relief seemed to pass over the room, a lessening of tension. Thank God, Signy said to herself, the baby's all right.

'Well done, Signy,' Dan murmured to her. 'That's great, keep it up. I could recommend you as an assistant surgeon.' He had his hand inside the uterus, loosening the placenta, then easing it out. At the same time the anaesthetist injected an IV drug to make the uterus contract and to keep bleeding to a minimum. The scrub nurse passed up a stainless-steel bowl for the large placenta.

Warmed by Dan's appreciation in spite of herself, she concentrated on what she had to do.

Later, he said to her, his head bent down close to hers as they were suturing the incision, 'Are you enjoying this?'

'Yes,' she said, her eyes meeting his briefly, 'this is my element.'

As though to complement her reply, the baby continued to fill the room with his lusty cries. When Signy allowed herself a quick glance at the resuscitation cart she could see his limbs waving about as he yelled, and that his skin had a healthy pink glow to it. She wanted to strip off her gown and gloves, to pick him up and cuddle him against her. He had, after all, endured much.

Later on, she walked back to Dan's cottage, grateful for the cool, fresh air on her face and arms. Wearing the comfortable trousers and blouse in which she'd travelled to Brookes Landing, she carried a light rain jacket with her.

It had been a satisfying day, finished off with an early supper in the hospital dining room with the other nurses in her group. Dan still had work to do and had told her to go on alone to the cottage. After the Caesarean section she had gone to see Clark Jakes, the man who had been attacked by the cougar, and had found that he was in a small acute-care unit off the men's surgical unit. He had been asleep, the sutured wounds on his face and neck uncovered to the air.

'How is he?' she'd said to a nurse in the unit.

'He's doing pretty well, except that he's traumatized, as you can imagine, having been attacked and nearly killed by a wild animal in an area where he's walked safely before,' the nurse had said. 'From now on, I guess he'll be much more aware and careful. There are places where he won't go without a shotgun.'

'I can imagine,' Signy had murmured, looking at the man's face, which was swollen around the eyes and in the areas of the wounds where the skin was purple and red from bruising. The black silk sutures looked like so many miniature train tracks here and there on his face and neck.

'We're doing what we can to prevent infection,' the nurse had said, indicating the intravenous line, 'and he's having anti-rabies shots just in case the animal was rabid. You never know. The other guy who was with him is a little worse off, he's in the intensive care unit. They'll both be all right, I'm sure.'

Signy nodded and went, the feeling very strong in her that here they were very close to raw nature, where man didn't always come off best in any confrontation. It was a sobering thought and it certainly cut one down to size…like Africa in many ways, yet different. Here, if you respected nature, understood it, took common-sense precautions, you could survive.

On the way to the lobby she met Sal, the nurse from the operating room.

'Hey, Signy!' Sal called to her.

'Hello,' she said, feeling how nice it was that people recognized her and called her by her name after such a short while in Brookes Landing, even though she had mixed feelings about talking to the chatty Sal.

'What happened?' Sal had said breathlessly, coming up to Signy with an avid expression on her face.

'Happened?' Signy said, mystified.

'With you and Dan Blake?' Sal said, glancing round her as though they had a conspiracy going. 'You did spend the night with him, didn't you?'

Signy laughed. 'Not in the way I think you mean,' she said. 'He let me sleep at his house.' She could imagine what Sal could do with the information if she told her that she had spent a good part of the night sleeping on a sofa, with Dan holding her hand. It would be all around the hospital, embellished, no doubt.

They parted without any significant exchange of information.

Now she enjoyed the walk, looked at the small, cosy houses nestled among conifers on quiet streets, separated and private from each other by the vegetation that surrounded them. The air was pure and scented with odours of moist soil and plants. There was moisture in the air, the promise of a gentle rain that kept the forests burgeoning with life.

At the cottage she changed into her nightclothes and robe so that she could put her clothes into Dan's washing machine, as he'd told her she could use it. Then she lit the log fire in the grate, which had been replenished by the woman who came in daily to clean Dan's house. It was fun, poking around the little cottage by herself, looking into cupboards, finding the things she needed to make herself a hot drink. She intended to have a long, luxurious bath, then sleep on the sofa by the fire before Dan came back.

Sitting with her hot drink, staring into the flames of the crackling fire which gave off an aromatic scent from an unknown wood, Signy acknowledged that for the first time in a long time she felt the glimmerings of something she could only call peace. The voices in her head, which had seemed to nag at her constantly, were silent, the images muted, toned down by the immediate scenes of mountains, wild woodland and dark, brooding trees nurtured on rain and by changing seasons. They seemed to have the power to blot out the arid plains of Africa, the memories of dry, hot winds.

The fire was still crackling when she woke up, and Signy had a sense that someone had put more logs on it. Immediately alert, she watched the firelight dance on the vaulted roof of the sitting room, where the massive rough-hewn beams were exposed. Someone was moving about in the kitchen.

She had intended to get up and dress before Dan came home, but it was obvious that she had slept on. It was dusk, and a light shone into the room from the kitchen.

She swung her feet down onto the wooden floor, on which colourful woven rag rugs were scattered here and there.

'Hi.' Dan stood in the doorway of the kitchen. 'I was just contemplating whether I should wake you to find out if you want supper.' He looked tired, serious, wearing utilitarian cotton trousers and an open-neck shirt.

There was something about his lean yet muscular frame that made him look as though he was ready to spring into action at any moment, Signy thought, whether it was to reach for a shotgun to fight off a wild animal or to jump into a vehicle to drive to the hospital at a moment's notice.

Looking at him, Signy doubted whether anything very much took him by surprise. She could also imagine that he could have his life planned down to the last detail almost and that, while he liked women and, no doubt, needed them to a certain extent, he would be very much in control of himself. That insight came to her swiftly, out of the blue, in those unguarded moments that often came to one after a refreshing sleep. Perhaps it was small wonder that he and the beautiful Marianne Crowley hadn't seen eye to eye. Signy also felt the irony of sharing a cottage with this man who had a strange link with her past.

Dan's eyes ran over her, from her mussed-up hair down over the robe to her bare feet. Involuntarily, his regard sent a rush of heat over her, and she instinctively pulled the robe closer around her body, castigating herself for not having woken sooner. She tried, by an act of will, not to let that flush reach her cheeks.

'I...um...I had supper at the hospital, thank you,' she said formally, pushing untidy stands of hair out of her eyes.

'A mug of hot chocolate, then?' he offered, lounging

against the doorframe, still looking at her intently, 'since it's a little cool now that the sun's gone.'

'That would be very nice.' She felt she had to force the words out. She was experiencing the odd feeling of trying to hate him for his part in what had happened in Africa yet admiring him for the work he did in this place. These ambivalent feelings were aroused in her because he was an attractive man, in spite of the twisted nose and the slightly gangsterish demeanour, as though he ought to have a gun in a holster slung low on his hip.

'I also want to talk to you about Dominic Fraser,' he said coolly, unexpectedly, 'because this appears to be the time and the place, since we're alone and not likely to be interrupted. We may not get another chance, and I want to get it out of the way. Perhaps...' his eyes went over her pointedly again '...you would prefer to get dressed before we discuss it.'

'Yes,' she agreed, standing up, gearing herself up mentally, honing her dislike.

Less than five minutes later, when she was dressed, her hair neat and sitting in a chair holding a mug of hot chocolate, Dan came and sat in another chair near her, though not near enough to make her feel that he was invading her personal space in any way. That was an odd thought, she mused, while commending him for what she perceived as his sensitivity. The thought also came to her that basically he probably didn't like her any more than she liked him.

'First, let me see if I have the facts straight,' he said, starting right into the topic. 'I want to get this over with before I get called into the hospital for something. And, by the way, Dr Crowley will be dropping by some time later for a drink because we have work issues to discuss. Would you like to join us?'

'Oh, no…thanks,' Signy said. 'I shall read and then sleep…or try to sleep.'

'Easier to sleep during the day on a sofa than it is at night?' he queried.

'Mmm.' She nodded.

'Let's see…you worked with Dr Fraser for about three months,' Dan said, 'then he and two other workers were taken hostage by a rebel group when they were away from the medical station in an area where they weren't supposed to be, an area that was considered unsafe by World Aid Doctors. They were exploring—for the adventure, I believe?'

Signy bit her lip, saying nothing. What he'd said was true.

'They were, fortunately, released unharmed about a week later,' he went on, fixing her with a shrewd glance. The matter-of-fact delivery was putting past events into perspective for her, even though she could feel herself fighting against any change in her own perceptions, having struggled for so long to sort it all out in her mind, to come to terms with it, with Dominic's actions.

'A month later, some UN workers were in the same general area,' Dan said. 'Dr Fraser took it upon himself to seek out these people in an attempt to see if he could get them to track down the rebels who had taken them hostage, even though the organization, the WAD, was doing all it could to get to the bottom of it. There wasn't much chance of success as they were most likely long gone. Dr Fraser left the medical station at a time when they could ill afford to be without one of their doctors. That was the last anyone at the station saw of him. Am I right so far?'

Signy nodded, feeling tears prick her eyes at the unemotional delivery of the facts. 'You've got it,' she said, refusing to be goaded by the implied criticism.

Giving her a hard stare, he went on. 'About a week later, WAD decided that the area of the medical station had become too dangerous and it was time to pull out, so they sent a truck to pick up the staff and take them out to a place of safety. Is that correct?'

'Yes.'

'When the truck arrived, without prior notice—which was difficult to give, communications being what they were—all the staff from WAD and WAN agreed to leave, except you, Ms Clover,' Dan said, his voice flat. 'Right?'

'Yes,' she said, returning his regard coolly. 'I didn't want to go without Dom—Dr Fraser, leaving him with no way to get out. I talked to the driver of the truck, who said he would send someone back in three or four days' time for me, and for…for Dr Fraser, if he'd returned by then.'

'So,' Dan went on relentlessly, 'one of our workers went there on a motorbike to get you, having an accident on the way. If Dr Fraser had been there, how do you think that three people could have got onto one motorbike?'

'Joachim said that he was prepared to stay at the medical station, with the African nurse there, that she would find a way for him to get out or to hide him if necessary. He was African, he knew the terrain, he knew the area.' Even to Signy's ears it sounded risky, rather lame. 'At the time,' she tried to explain, 'in a time of desperation, it seemed as good a solution as any. It's easy for us to sit here in cold blood and pull it all apart…as though we had a lot of options.'

'I'm just trying to elicit the facts,' he said unemotionally.

'It's not my way to abandon people,' she said.

'Even if your actions endanger others?'

'It was a risk I was willing to take. I didn't have time to ponder it,' she said.

He just sat and looked at her, his expression giving nothing away.

'I think I hate you,' she said calmly, not having planned to say that, watching his eyebrows rise sardonically above his shrewd eyes that seemed to read everything about her. 'It wasn't all cut and dried like that. We had to make decisions on the spur of the moment in that primitive place, and hope that we'd made the right ones.' There was no way she was going to let him get away with sitting there as judge and jury. 'And what, Dr Blake, was your part in all this?'

'I simply passed on the directive to get out—I didn't make it,' he said. 'I put it in writing, I arranged for the truck and driver, as I was directed to do. I didn't hear till later that one person hadn't come out and one was missing. I wasn't responsible for sorting it all out.'

With her hands clenched on the mug, Signy faced him. 'It was a calculated risk that I stayed behind,' she said. 'Like so many other things in life.'

A few tears had fallen from her eyes and run down her cheeks. They were tears for Dominic. 'I loved Dominic,' she said. 'He was a good person. I could no more leave him behind than I could leave a brother.'

His loaded silence seemed calculated to bring home to her that Dominic was gone for ever.

'You make Dr Fraser sound like a naughty boy who went off on an adventure that he shouldn't have gone on. He'd been taken hostage, he wanted justice done for that,' she said.

'Justice?' Dan gave a dry laugh. 'There are no such things as justice and human rights in a place where order has broken down, where the infrastructure isn't in place to mete out justice. It's just an empty word.'

'All the more reason why we have to look after our own,' she countered.

'Yes...but the key is appropriate behaviour. In many ways he behaved like a boy,' Dan went on relentlessly. 'As though he were on an adventure or something, going out of the designated safe area, instead of being a member of a team sent there for a designated purpose.'

Signy didn't reply.

'A few days after you left, the medical station was set on fire and burned to the ground by the so-called rebels,' he said, stating a fact.

'Yes,' she said, as tears dripped onto her clenched hands. 'But that's not the end of the story, Dr Blake.' She looked up at him. 'The mourning goes on.'

There was an unreadable expression on his face as they stared at each other.

'I don't care if you think I was wrong, if you think I'm weak...I don't care what you think,' she said quietly. 'Who are you to judge me? I think you would agree that you can't go on second-guessing yourself. I did what I thought was right at the time. And I don't care if you put in a bad report about me to the WAN headquarters. As you said yourself, sometimes you don't have very long in which to make a decision.'

The fire crackled comfortingly, while outside the wind stirred the branches of trees. They sat and looked at each other. Signy vowed that she wouldn't be the first to avert her eyes.

The sound of quick footsteps on the wooden verandah, followed by a sharp ring of the doorbell, cut across the mesmerizing silence. Signy jumped, almost dropping the mug which she still held tightly in her lap. Dan slowly got up, seeming to unfold himself, and walked towards the door. Apparently he wasn't fast enough for the person who stood outside because the bell pealed again twice, impatiently, imperiously. That would be Marianne Crowley.

Swiftly Signy made her escape, heading for the sanctuary of the small guest room, where she closed the door.

CHAPTER SIX

SIGNY sat on the bed, then got up again agitatedly and began to pace the room, passing a hand over her forehead repeatedly.

Dan's words had disturbed her, his bald reiteration of the story. Yet at the same time, in the core of her being, a sense of hard, sobering reality was taking shape, as though she was at last seeing the past as the past, unchangeable. There was a sense of placing it where it belonged, rather than have it dominating the present as it had done for so long. She supposed this was what was called coming to terms with something.

She was going to stand by what she had just said, that she'd made the decisions she had because to her there had been no alternative. As she'd said, she wasn't going to second-guess herself. There was no point. In a similar situation, she would make a decision in light of the circumstances of that time.

The room seemed claustrophobic, she wanted to get out. Quickly she pulled on a sweater that she had in her overnight bag, then put the rain jacket over it. It would be nice to get out for some air, to walk while she sorted out her thoughts.

Listening at the door, not wanting to butt into the meeting between Dan and his former girlfriend, she waited. There had been animated conversation and short bursts of laughter coming from the sitting room. Marianne had a loud voice, seemed to be one of those forceful women who thought she had to constantly keep her end up, otherwise some man would get the better of her. Maybe that wasn't fair, Signy conceded. She didn't really know the woman. Not loud and pushy herself, she was mystified by those who were, assuming it came from a basic lack of self-assurance, not its opposite.

When she judged that they had moved to the study or kitchen…or perhaps the bedroom…she left her room and crossed the sitting room to let herself out the main door.

The evening was pleasantly cool, a gentle wind blowing, bringing the scents of the north with it. Signy began to walk, going along the narrow road towards the hospital, having a vague idea that she would stay within the confines of the small town, where she wasn't likely to encounter any dangerous wild animals. The physical activity would tire her out, help her to sleep later. Walking always helped her to clear her head. There seemed to be no one else about and she welcomed the solitude as she walked under the tall cedar trees that lined the streets between the houses.

After about fifteen minutes a light rain began to fall.

A sound must have woken her later in the night, as her eyelids sprang open and she found herself wide awake and alert. For two or three seconds she didn't know where she was then, as the dim outline of the room took shape, the emotions associated with the evening before came flooding over her. Forcing herself to relax, she lay there to think about all that had happened in the short time that she'd been in this part of the world. Her bedside clock told her that it was 3 a.m.

Knowing that she would probably not fall asleep again, she decided to get up and read, maybe make herself a hot drink. This was better than having bad dreams, she thought wryly as she got up and put on her own dressing-gown.

The floor creaked a bit as she crept across the sitting room to get to the kitchen, where she put on a side light rather than the main light. Dan needed sleep more than she did. Trying not to make much noise, she got together the things she needed to make a cup of tea.

Waking early, persistently, was a sign of clinical depression, she mused. Well, she didn't think she was suffering from that, even though her spirits had been low. Stress, with the anxiety that it produced, could bring about the same effect, she presumed.

Perhaps talking to Dan had, after all, started the healing process, because now the sense continued that things were very slowly beginning to move on. She was reluctant to concede that he might have helped her. Really, she hated him...the sooner she could get back to Kelp Island and away from his house, the better. Friday couldn't come soon enough for her. From now on she could avoid him a lot of the time if she really wanted to. As Terri had said, he did seem to arrange things so that they were together, so that he could watch her. Well, she would speak to Max about spending more time with him.

As was often the case when you were trying to be careful, she dropped the metal lid of the teapot into the stainless-steel sink with a loud clatter. 'Oh, hell!' she muttered, picking it up quickly. Then she hastily poured boiling water onto a teabag in the pot.

The last thing she wanted was to wake up Dan. Perhaps Dr Crowley was with him. The thought came to her, unbidden. She didn't suppose that he led a celibate life. That prospect exasperated her inexplicably, perhaps because it made her feel like an interloper in his house.

While she waited for the tea to steep for a few minutes,

with her arms folded across her chest in an unconsciously protective gesture, Dan walked silently into the room.

'Oh…oh,' Signy said, taking a step back. 'Did I wake you? I hope not. I…woke up and couldn't get back to sleep, so I've made tea. I hope that's all right.' She backed away from him so that she was up against the work counter.

'It's quite all right,' he said, coming into the centre of the small room, looking rumpled in his dressing-gown, as though he might have slept in it. 'No, you didn't exactly wake me, I was having trouble sleeping anyway. I heard you moving about.'

'Sorry,' she mumbled. 'Would you like some tea? It's just about ready.'

'Thanks,' he said.

Simultaneously they moved to get another mug out of the cupboard above the sink and their shoulders touched. 'Oh,' she said again, recoiling. 'Um…do you prefer a mug or a cup?' At any other time she might have laughed hysterically at the mundane nature of their verbal exchange.

Dan ran a hand through his hair. With his hair untidy, he looked somehow more human, she thought; less of a judgmental doctor, more of a man…just a man.

'Let me get it, Signy,' he said, turning to her. Somehow the use of her name made her sort of melt inside and become vulnerable, as though she would cry at the drop of a hat. She wanted to move away from him but felt oddly leaden, as though her legs wouldn't work. They looked at each other and she tried to put all the dislike she felt for him into her eyes.

He reached up a hand to take a mug out of the cupboard, then stilled. Instead of grasping it, he put his hand around the back of her neck, the warm fingers moving into her hair.

Signy held her breath and felt her whole body stiffen as his touch seemed like a current of electricity moving through her. His gaze held hers for a moment and he frowned slightly, as though puzzled by her, then his eyes moved down to rest on her mouth. Involuntarily her lips parted slightly.

As though in slow motion, his head came down to her, giving her plenty of opportunity to get away, and his lips covered hers. A small moan formed deep in her throat. She didn't know whether it was a sound of protest or one of acknowledgement of something…something that she needed. All she knew then was that her eyes closed of their own volition and her awareness excluded everything else but the warmth of Dan's firm mouth on hers, the surge of recognition throughout her body…the recognition that he was an attractive man…and the unmistakable response of sexual desire like a tide sweeping over her. It was one that she could no more control than the actual tide.

Very slowly but inevitably, Dan turned completely round to her, his mouth still on hers, and drew her into his arms, the length of his firm, lean body pressing warmly against hers. Signy thought she might faint with the unexpectedness of it, the revelation of her own response. Her heart was pounding, as though someone were banging a drum in her ear. Although she didn't put her arms around him, she wanted to…she wanted to.

All she could do was stand there as though paralysed, like an idiot, she thought wildly. It was too ridiculous! She didn't even like him. They had little in common, even though they came essentially from the same country and background, shared jobs in the same profession, belonged to the same organization.

He took his mouth from hers and gently kissed her neck, her ear, her cheek. 'Signy…' He murmured her name, and to her horror she felt herself literally go weak at the knees, something she had only read about in stories, something she hadn't even experienced with Simon, whom she had loved.

She ought to push him away, she told herself, but instead she put her arms around his waist as she felt herself become unsteady. Again he kissed her on the mouth. This was utter madness. His hand touched the back of her neck, his fingers in her hair, holding her to him so that he could kiss her more deeply. She was, in a moment, completely lost in him.

Simultaneously they pulled apart. Signy swallowed convulsively, her whole body tingling with nervous tension as they looked at each other. To her, he looked somewhat stunned, while she knew that she must have an expression of muted shock, bordering on horror, on her face. A few hours ago she'd told him that she hated him, while he'd looked as though he couldn't have cared less.

Letting out a pent-up breath on a sigh, he said, 'I didn't intend that to happen.'

Struggling for control and an appearance of sophistication, she said, 'No, I don't suppose you did. Neither did I.'

Distractedly, Dan reached for another mug, then carefully poured them both tea, while she stood trying to compose herself. She couldn't think of what to say next and it appeared that he couldn't either. Silently he pushed the sugar bowl a few inches along the counter in her direction and handed her the tea. She nodded her thanks.

When he sighed again and leaned against the counter,

she took it to be a gesture of abject regret. The tiny room, with him in it, became as claustrophobic as her bedroom had been, so she took her tea and walked out to the sitting room, where the fire still glowed red. Desperate for a distracting task, she busied herself putting more kindling on the embers, then a small log. Then she sat hunched in the semi-darkness on the sofa, her hands cupping the hot mug. The immediacy of this man, his touch, his kiss, had pushed Simon and Dominic out of the forefront of her mind.

Aware that Dan was looking at her from the doorway, she didn't look up. What on earth were they going to say to each other? Not usually at a complete loss for words, she felt oddly mute, as though words were somehow inadequate.

Sensitive to his movements, she noted that he went over to the CD player and soft classical music filled the void, the nostalgic sweep of violins. Yes, that was perfect, she thought with an inward, tremulous sigh. The sound suited her mood perfectly. Now we don't have to speak, she thought, relieved. Slowly she felt herself relax and sipped her tea. Even when Dan came to sit at the other end of the long sofa, putting his feet up comfortably on a stool, she felt all right. It was as though the music united them and yet formed a barrier at the same time, each able to retreat into a private fantasy world created by it.

When it had come to an end, he said, 'I hope you don't hate me too much.'

Casting around for an answer, she came up with the only thing she could say. 'I don't know,' she said, her voice small.

He put on more music. In the few moments that he was away, she readjusted her position so that she sat with her legs curled up comfortably underneath her, with several cushions supporting her back. Knowing she wouldn't be able to sleep if she went back to bed, at least she might be able to doze here in front of the fire until it was time to get up.

When she had finished the tea she resolutely closed her eyes, letting the music fill her mind, trying to blot out her very acute awareness that Dan sat a few feet away from her. It was sobering that she hadn't disliked being kissed by him.

The next morning, having slept after all on the sofa, she found that Dan had already gone out and had left a note for her in the kitchen. It said that she and Terri should report to the emergency department at the hospital at ten o'clock, where they would meet Max, who would spend the day there with them.

Signy found that she had mixed feelings about spending the day with Max, yet her predominant one was of an odd sort of relief. In the note Dan reminded her that they would be returning to Kelp Island on Friday. Since it was only eight o'clock, she had two hours in which to shower, have breakfast and get herself over to the hospital.

As she went through the routine of getting ready for work she pondered the apparent fact that she was gradually making a shift from her former life to the present one. The image of Simon, with his fair good looks, the golden youth that he had seemed to be, was becoming dimmer in her mind's eye. They both seemed to her now to have been so naïve, to have given no thought to what they would do, how or where they would live, if they decided to break up and dissolve their mutual home.

With Dominic, the change was less, but change there was. A momentary sense of disloyalty assailed her, before the realization that she had done everything she could have done, to the point perhaps of stupidity, to help Dominic in his hour of need. Where others had left, she had remained. There had been nothing more she could have done.

Perhaps she'd had an over-developed sense of responsibility for Dominic. That was really absurd, because he had been an adult, older than her. He should have known what he'd been doing, the extent of the risks he'd taken. For his part, he might have known that others in the team would put themselves at risk for him. Still, she didn't feel like thanking Dan for pointing it out because she wasn't sure of his motives.

Signy sighed as she drank coffee and dried her hair with her hair-dryer at the same time. When her hair was dry, soft and fluffy, she applied a little make-up to her face. It was her intention to get to the hospital early so that she could meet up, maybe, with other members of her group in the hospital dining room. Sharing a cottage with Dan was making her life a little too intense. She wanted the company of female colleagues for a while.

Unfortunately, the first person to greet her as she sat down in the dining room with another cup of coffee, with none of her colleagues in sight, was Sal.

'Hi! Signy!' The ebullient Sal sat down with her. 'How are you? And...' she leaned forward conspiratorially '...more to the point, how is the gorgeous Dan?'

It took will-power for Signy not to blush before those gimlet eyes as she had a vision of herself in Dan's arms, then curled up on a sofa, with him at the other end of it. What fun Sal would have with that! It would be all around the hospital, embellished with lurid detail, in no time at all.

'I hardly see him,' she said airily, 'so I wouldn't know. He leads a hectic life.'

'You know, I was beginning to think that he and Marianne Crowley were going to get together again,' Sal said, 'because they seemed to be spending a lot of time together. But I reckon he's not ready to make a commitment—he seems to be backing off again. He seems to be one of those guys who's got his life all mapped out, and he won't let himself fall for a woman a moment sooner that he's planned. You know the type.'

Signy nodded.

'Maybe he'll be one of those guys who waits till he's about forty-five, then he'll marry a twenty-two-year-old girl who's besotted with him, get her to have three or four kids, one after the other, to make up for lost time. Then one day she wakes up and realizes that she's married to an old man and that she hasn't had any fun, and isn't likely to.' Sal gave a cackling laugh. 'Then she decides to divorce him, and he fights her like hell, with his age and money to back him up, for custody of the kids. And she hasn't got any work experience behind her.'

It was impossible to be annoyed with her, so Signy grinned back. 'You missed your vocation. You should be writing scripts for soap operas.'

'Maybe I should at that.' Sal laughed. 'But I'm talking about real life. There's nothing fictitious about that scenario, believe you me. It's so predictable, it's pathetic. Yet those women act surprised when it happens to them. You coming to the OR today?'

'No, it's the emergency department, with Max Seaton.'

'Oh!' Sal raised her eyes in ecstasy. 'Could I tell you a thing or two about Max Seaton!'

Signy groaned and rose to her feet. 'Please, don't,' she said. 'Must go.'

Terri was already there when she got to the department, as were Pearl and Max. They greeted her like one long lost.

'We're going to look around to get ourselves orientated to this place,' Pearl explained. 'Then we'll wait at the front desk here to see what comes our way.'

'Sounds good to me,' Signy said.

She found herself wondering where Dan was working today. Perhaps from now on he would avoid her as much as the job allowed. Well, that was quite all right with her, she told herself as the three of them began an exploration of the small yet very efficient-looking emergency department. She would be doing the same thing.

'I want to go up some time today to see those two men who were attacked by the cougar,' Signy said to Terri. 'Just to see how they're progressing. Do you want to come?'

'Yep. I went last night. They both look in a bit of a mess, black and blue and with all the sutures, but the wounds don't seem to be getting infected,' Terri said. 'I expect they'll stay in here for a while.'

On Friday, as planned, the small group of nurses prepared to go back to Kelp Island. Signy hadn't worked again directly with Dan, and on the Friday morning she found herself saying goodbye to him at the cottage and formally thanking him for letting her stay there. Even as she said the words, she felt the irony in them as Dan looked at her with a certain expression on his face that told her they wouldn't have found themselves in a compromising situation if he hadn't invited her to stay there, which he now regretted. His manner clearly indicated that the intention hadn't been there from the beginning. As for herself, she found that she couldn't make eye contact with him for more than few seconds without a flush staining her cheeks.

'I expect to be back on the island myself on Sunday evening,' he said. 'On Monday and Tuesday you'll be getting some instruction from either me or Max, then you'll be coming back to Brookes Landing from time to time, and maybe some smaller communities even farther up the coast.'

'That will be nice,' she said sincerely. 'I've enjoyed being here, it's been an interesting experience.'

'Good,' he said, with a voice that to her sounded cold.

It was good to be back on the island, in the yellow and pink room that she was coming to think of as hers, a place she would be sorry to leave. Maybe in the future she would paint her next bedroom yellow and pink, if it belonged to her. The other women in Moose Head hut gathered for tea and then retired to catch up on mail of all types and to rest.

Signy went to Reception to see Sabrina, and found that there were four letters for her from her parents and friends. On the way her eyes turned to Holly Berry, standing on the opposite side of the clearing by itself, where Dan stayed when he was in residence. The unlived-in look of the place gave her an odd feeling, a momentary sense of the isolation of the island, surrounded as it was by the vast ocean. Maybe, she told herself, she felt that way because he was one of the few people she knew in the place, not because she missed him or liked him. Beggars couldn't be choosers.

Back in her room she checked her e-mails, and spent some time sending messages. After putting a note under Terri's door, asking her if she wanted to go for a walk to a beach later, she fell asleep on the bed. It was easier to sleep during the day when a comforting light came through the window and her eyes could light on familiar objects before she allowed herself to drift away.

When she got up again, Terri had put a note under her door saying that, yes, she would love to go for a walk and that they should bear in mind the need to get back before dusk. She suggested a time to meet in the sitting area of the hut.

Signy got her things together—her clothes, her survival gear, the flashlight, the alarm and whistle, the cellphone, the map, a bar of chocolate and a bottle of water in a knapsack.

'There seems to be a touch of autumn in the air,' Terri commented later as they trudged along a path in the woods, going at quite a fast pace. 'Some of the leaves are changing colour and some have fallen.'

'That's it, I think,' Signy said, walking closely behind Terri. 'More of these trees are deciduous than I thought at first, though the conifers seemed to dominate.'

When they finally burst out of the woods onto the beach area, confronted by the breathtaking spectacle of the rolling surf, they sat down under a tree to rest, hugging their knees, sheltered there from the stiff breeze that whipped at their clothing.

'I'm glad you suggested this walk, Signy,' Terri said after a few minutes, 'because I want to talk to someone. I feel that if I don't talk I'm going to burst, and I know you're a good listener and wouldn't repeat what's said to you. Of course, if you'd rather not be my confidante, just say so. I wouldn't want to burden you with it otherwise. And if you feel the need to talk, maybe we can be of some help to each other.'

Signy nodded, looking sideways in commiseration at

the young woman whom she now considered a friend, finding it hard to realize that they had only known each other for a short time. There was the familiarity between them of their shared work background. That counted for a lot.

Terri's short, spiky hair was blowing in the wind, as was her own.

'You want to talk about East Timor?' she asked.

'Yes.'

'I don't know whether I'll be of much help to you,' Signy said honestly. 'I'll try. I know that just listening helps, and I can listen. Shall we walk along the beach a bit first, then we'll find another quiet spot.'

They held their faces up to the sky, letting the blustery wind catch them in its embrace. It seemed to blow away the past, here in this primal place that seemed to bear no memory of man, where raw nature reigned supreme because it was mightier than puny man—arbitrary, totally impersonal.

'This place cuts one down to size, doesn't it?' Signy said, letting herself go with the feeling. 'It's a place without much human history.' For hundreds of years it had been held in the roar of the mighty sea. It was a place of dramatic storms, earthquakes out to sea, the threat of earthquakes on land. 'It's so different from Africa...the birthplace of mankind.'

'Yeah.'

When they sat down to talk, Signy had already made up her mind that she would listen to Terri and then she would tell her about Simon and Dominic—not so much about Africa and work as about her mixed-up emotions, her all-pervading sadness.

On the return journey through the forest they walked quickly, not wanting to find themselves among the trees at dusk, the place already being gloomy. They both felt emotionally heightened yet oddly at peace for having talked to each other, woman to woman.

'I've been wanting to ask you something,' Terri said, puffing a bit as they drew abreast on a wider section of the path, not slackening their pace. 'You can tell me to mind my own business if you like, but I'm curious. You know you said that Dr Blake was spending a fair amount of time with you because he wants to watch you, see how you shape up?'

'Mmm,' Signy said, out of breath. 'Ooh, I must be less fit than I thought, I'm really puffed.'

'I think he likes you,' Terri went on. 'Seriously. Yes, he does watch you, but to me it doesn't look the way you say—it seems to me that it's the interest of a man in a woman. Pure and simple. I thought I would mention it in the light of what you've just told me about those two other guys in your past. Maybe you can't see it because of them.'

'Oh, I don't think so, Terri,' she protested, thinking that a kiss didn't necessarily mean much when a man and a woman were in close proximity. It was almost an accident, not premeditated. 'I don't think he really likes me. Why would he, when he hardly knows me and I'm one of a group? There must already be a lot of women in this part of the world who are just waiting to get even a hint from him that he's available. Our friend Sal is a case in point.'

'Oh, she should get out more,' Terri said, laughing.

'Anyway, I really can't stand him,' Signy went on. 'Oh, he's a good doctor all right, a very good teacher, a man of integrity, probably very reliable in the field…brave, I expect, a nice enough man, if you like that sort of thing.'

'Why can't you stand him?' Terri said, looking at her

curiously. 'I think he's a really nice bloke…even with that nose.' She laughed again. 'In fact, it sort of adds something to him.'

'Yes, it does,' Signy admitted, smiling. 'He's so…sort of too self-contained….I can't really explain it… You feel that in every situation he would be right on top of things.'

'What's wrong with that?'

'I don't know—except that maybe he would make you feel inadequate.'

'Better than the anxiety of being with someone you suspect, or know, will let you down most of the time. Maybe you're attracted to boys in adult bodies, Signy.' Terri laughed to lighten her insight, and Signy joined in, a little uncomfortably.

'Perhaps.'

'Many a true word spoken in jest,' Terri added. 'Dan's all man, but not macho with it—or arrogant. That's pretty rare.'

'True,' Signy conceded, more disturbed by Terri's comments than she knew how to deal with at that moment.

'Maybe you're scared of a real man because you think you can't cope. Maybe someone like him is just what you need,' Terri said. 'An affair with him, short and sweet, would put those two other guys in their place pretty quickly. You say he doesn't like you. Well, I suspect you could make him more than like you without too much trouble. After all, we'll be out of here before anything too heavy could develop. This isn't a place where we can hang about.'

'One can get too heavy pretty quickly,' Signy said doubtfully, and they both burst out laughing. 'Although I don't think that would be the case with Dan.'

Don't be so sure, a small voice in her own mind warned her. In quiet moments she found herself mulling over the feel of him when he'd held her, his firm mouth on hers. In her conversation with Terri she hadn't told her about that, and now the omission made her feel awkward. A flush came to her face, adding to the flush of physical exertion.

'This is ridiculous, Terri,' she said.

'Don't just dismiss it, Signy. I'm serious.'

After a few minutes they both started to chuckle again. 'You know, I'm glad we talked. I feel light-hearted, as though I can't stop laughing,' Terri said.

'Same here.'

'Let's have a glass of wine when we get back. I've got some stashed away. Don't forget what I said about Dan. He would be good for you. I fully intend to have a little dalliance with Max. I know just where I am with him.'

Struck dumb by this remark, Signy—who was a couple of paces ahead—grinned at Terri and set out at a faster pace.

CHAPTER SEVEN

IT WAS really great to have some time off again, to walk, to sleep, to talk to the other nurses, to send messages by computer to the outside world. Signy, along with the others, made notes and did reading that had been assigned to them as part of the course.

On Sunday evening, Signy noted that Dan must have arrived when she saw lights on in his hut. Later he appeared in the mess hut for supper with them. She didn't sit with him or speak to him. It seemed to her that he was making a point of avoiding her, which was successful, and she was doing the same with him.

For the whole of the next week they had lectures, informal talks, seminars and discussion groups about safety and strategies in the field. Some of these activities were conducted by Max or Dan, still others by visiting lecturers who came to the island for one day at a time. Dan wasn't there continuously as he had to get back to Brookes Landing to see his patients and to help with emergencies. During these absences Signy felt herself relax, she wasn't sure exactly why. Yet whenever she left Moose Head, she found her eyes going to Holly Berry, searching it for signs of occupation.

On Saturday, Signy and her colleagues in Moose Head discovered that they would be going back to Brookes Landing on the following Monday, for perhaps the whole week, and also would visit some smaller settlements farther up the coast where there were nursing stations and doctors called once in a while.

Later that day, after lunch, Signy slipped away quickly, wanting to walk by herself through the woods to the beach, to look at the ocean once again close up and to overcome her residual fear of being alone in the forest. As time went by, she was finding a certain peace here. Physical activity in the open air helped.

The climate was changing now that they were at the end of the second week in October. The evenings and mornings were becoming darker, there was more rain and mist, the leaves on the trees were falling gradually.

After the long, brisk walk through the forest and then along the beach, she found herself glorying in the sound of the ocean and the wind. Huge strands of kelp lay here and there, further out from where she was walking close to the trees; they looked black on the pale sand, lonely and abandoned.

As she turned her back into the wind, facing the way she had come, she saw a man come out of the trees by a different path from the one she had taken, stopping her in her tracks, a momentary fear assailing her. This was a very isolated place. There was no one on this island un-accounted for, so she had been told, and much of the coastline wasn't easily accessible to boats.

The man waved. In a few moments, while she stood still, she saw that it was Dan. A gamut of emotions washed over her, as well as a wave of heat as she let out a pent-up breath and began to walk forward slowly again in his direction, her predominant feeling, to her surprise, being one of a peculiar kind of relief.

'Signy! Signy!' he was calling to her, shouting to make himself heard.

'Hello!' she called back, waving. As the gap closed

between them, she inadvertently thought of the remarks
Terri had made to her about an affair with Dan—short
and sweet, as she'd put it. How did Terri know that it
would be sweet? she wondered, a peculiar hysteria taking
hold of her as they drew closer. He had seen her at her
most vulnerable, which lent a peculiar kind of intimacy
to their interaction now, as well as making her feel at a
disadvantage with him. Momentarily she wondered
whether she should disappear among the trees to avoid
him…but she didn't want to…

'Hi,' he said, coming up to her, his casual clothing, dark
green rain jacket and hair whipped by the wind, colour in
his face. 'How are you?' His lean face, with its square-
cut jaw, the laughter lines around the eyes, was becoming
very familiar to her.

'All right, thank you,' she said, feeling a little wary, as
his attitude to her when they'd last been alone had been
cool, or so it had seemed to her. Again, Terri's words
came back to her, something about Dan being all man,
mature. 'I…didn't know you would be here,' she added
somewhat unnecessarily, on the defensive, not wanting
him to think that she had engineered a meeting.

'Otherwise you wouldn't have come?' he queried, grinning in that rather wry way he had.

Signy flushed. 'Perhaps not.'

'Well,' he said, 'I *did* know you were going to be here.
I saw your name and route in the check-out book in the
office. I came on a different path, as I didn't want you to
think I was dogging your footsteps. Let's walk.' He
touched her arm lightly.

They battled the wind together for minutes without
speaking.

'You know,' he said at length, as they came to a halt
beside a particularly large and long piece of kelp that had

been washed up closer to the forest, 'there's another meaning for kelp. It's kelpie, actually…from Scottish lore. A kelpie is a water spirit that usually comes in the form of a horse. It's reputed to delight in ensnaring and drowning travellers.'

'Oh…really?' Signy looked around her, noting that while her attention had been on Dan a fine white mist had crept in from the sea, over the sand close to the water, like a low cloud, bringing with it a greater coolness. When she looked out to the ocean she could see the white-capped waves, like the proverbial prancing horses, coming into the shore relentlessly through the mist, and she shivered. 'I wish you hadn't said that,' she added, looking at him accusingly. 'I shan't be able to get that out of my mind now when I look at the water.'

When he grinned slowly and ruefully at her, something happened to her concept of him as not being her type, and something happened to the habitual antagonism that was always just below the surface of her consciousness. Maybe he wasn't her type, she told herself, but she could quite see how some other women might find him irresistible, especially when he smiled like that.

'Myths often serve a purpose, they can mimic reality,' he said. 'This one makes sure that we don't underestimate the power of the sea.'

'This mist…' she began, looking at it as it swirled around their legs.

'Yes, we ought to start back,' he said, 'while we can still find the path easily. Come on.' They turned back. 'It will be clear in the woods, and somewhat warmer.'

As though on cue, it began to rain quite suddenly as they walked back to the Huckleberry path, then in seconds it had become a downpour. Signy pulled the hood of her jacket up. This was why moss clung to the trees, why everything grew so abundantly.

When Dan took her hand and began to run, pulling her after him, she didn't resist. In the woods the rain was less, but still heavy. Panting for breath, they pushed their way under a giant fir tree, whose branches swept low to the ground in graceful curves. Underneath it, near the trunk, it was possible for a person to stand up.

'We'll shelter here for a bit until the worst is over,' Dan said. He lowered himself, his back to the large trunk, onto the dry ground which was covered with brown needles from the tree. Under there it was almost dark. 'It should slacken off in about fifteen minutes.'

'Should we be under a tree if there's a storm?' she asked, looking up at the trunk and branches towering above them, through which a few drops of water fell on her face. 'What if it get's struck by lightning?'

'There isn't going to be a storm,' he said, 'not that sort of storm.'

'How do you know?' she asked obstinately, looking at him through the gloom.

'I just know,' he said, a slight smile on his face as he looked up at her. 'Come and sit down here. We'll wait it out.'

Even though she essentially disliked Dan, she told herself yet again, her heart was beating fast as she lowered herself to the ground near him. It was quieter here, just the drumming of rain on foliage higher above them. She pulled her jacket more closely around her, drew up her knees and folded her arms over them, hugging them to her chest to keep warm. 'It's amazing how quickly the temperature has changed,' she said.

'Yeah,' he agreed. 'That's why you always have to

wear warm clothing and suitable boots. Sit closer to me.'
They both moved a little so that they sheltered each other.

Why am I doing this? What's happening to me? Almost
angrily, Signy addressed herself, wondering why she obediently shifted close to him, feeling her control of the
situation slipping away from her. Maybe Terri was right.
She wasn't used to dealing with a man like Dan
Blake…hard, in complete command of himself and the
situation.

'Why did you seek me out?' she demanded, trying to
take back some of the initiative.

'I wanted to see you alone as we haven't had any opportunity all week,' he said, putting his head back against
the trunk of the tree. 'We parted on a rather odd note, so
I wanted to see how you are…in the light of the fact that
you had all those bad dreams when you were staying at
my place. Thinking it over, I want to apologize, too, for
being so touchy on one or two occasions. I have to put
that down to the fact that I was under a certain amount
of strain with some of the cases I had, as well as the
pressure of other work. Nevertheless, that's no excuse,
really. I don't want you to think I'm a complete boor.'

'I don't,' she said truthfully. 'I don't know what I
think.' She paused, uncommonly aware of him, searching
her mind for something to say. 'Actually, the dreams are
getting fewer, and the ones I do have are less upsetting
and dramatic.'

'I'm no expert on dreams,' he said laconically, although
Signy had the sense that he was more tense than he appeared, 'but I would say that you're coming to terms with
a few things, finally getting them sorted out.'

'Perhaps,' she said. 'I like being on this island. I can't
really say why. It's an escape of sorts, I suppose. It's the
smallness of it, so manageable.'

'Mmm. Maybe now would be a good time to talk about a few things,' he suggested, 'if you want to. There's no coercion.'

'No?' Signy laughed ironically. 'When you've got me trapped here under a tree in a rainstorm?'

Again he smiled that slow smile at her, and shrugged. 'You're free to go,' he said. 'I just hope you won't.'

Unable to sustain eye contact, Signy picked up a twig from the ground and proceeded to break it into tiny pieces to distract herself. 'Terri and I talked about our respective situations, about our field work,' she said quickly, the words tumbling out, while she wished that he wouldn't look at her. 'It helped a lot.' She turned to him. 'Why don't you tell me about yourself?' she suggested challengingly. 'I feel more at ease giving confidences if they're returned. It somehow evens the score.'

'You're right, of course,' he said, sitting with his hands hanging casually between his drawn-up knees.

'Tell me about Marianne Crowley,' she ventured softly.

Dan gave a dry laugh. 'Our mutual friend Sal has been talking,' he commented.

'Yes.'

'Well…' He took in a deep breath and let it out slowly. 'Marianne and I were what you might call an item at one time. That was mainly, I can see now, because we were thrown together in Brookes Landing with our work. There aren't that many beautiful female doctors up in those out-of-the-way places.'

'Go on.' Signy wasn't sure why she was goading him, why she had a genuine desire to know, except that she was fed up with always being the one under the microscope, so to speak.

'To cut a long story short…'

'Why?'

Again he laughed. 'It would bore you. It's really a dull story. I didn't love her enough to have bad dreams. She didn't like me being away from time to time with World Aid Doctors, for one thing, and she didn't want to come with me. What she wanted was marriage, to have homes in Vancouver and Brookes Landing, to settle down to a quiet professional and family life. I wasn't ready for that. Neither did I want to give up any of my work. I guess it provides something that I need.'

Signy nodded, looking at him quickly then away again.

'I want to share my expertise with the less fortunate of the world,' he went on, 'to teach other health-care workers in those places to have greater knowledge so that they can be more self-sufficient. We—Marianne and I—agreed to differ, and parted.'

'That was what you wanted?'

'Yes.'

'And do you care now?'

'No. It's all sort of blown over, you might say,' he said thoughtfully. 'I can see now that we were together because of our easy proximity, not because there was much else to it…not as much as there should have been for a permanent relationship. So far, she hasn't found anybody else who will fulfil her ambitions, although she wants to, I suspect.' To Signy, the tone of his voice suggested that his heart hadn't been broken by the decision.

'And you?'

'I've decided that I can't afford to get involved yet— that is, can't take the time. I've too many other commitments.' It was stated unemotionally, rather as he'd said that the rain would slacken off in fifteen minutes.

'What about…your own personal needs?' she ventured.

He shrugged. 'I get by,' he said.

They were silent for a while, listening to the patter of

rain and the sudden louder pounding of surf in the near distance. Again Signy shivered, thinking of the water sprites.

'The kelpies are riding,' he said.

'Oh, don't!'

Dan put an arm round her, drawing her shoulder against his. 'Cold?'

'Mmm,' she said, her heart giving an unexpected lurch as she reluctantly felt the pull of his attraction. 'And thinking of the long walk back.' What on earth am I doing here—with him? she asked herself furiously. It was as though her mind and body had become split and her body was responding to its own urgent needs, was getting the better of her.

Again Dan sighed, putting his head back against the rough bark of the trunk and closing his eyes. Signy glanced at his profile, his face so close to hers.

Without moving or opening his eyes, he said softly, 'Signy, I want to kiss you… I want to hold you in my arms.'

Instantly her heart leapt again, sending a rush of blood to her face, and her throat felt tight as though she wouldn't be able to speak if she tried. Every part of her body was intensely aware of his so close to her, his side against hers…in spite of the fact that he wasn't her type. Not enough like a boy? And therefore not manageable? The words tantalized her, the ideas that Terri had put into her head so provocatively.

When she didn't answer after a few seconds, he turned his head slowly to look at her, his eyes meeting hers. Even in the gloom it wasn't difficult to see the desire that was naked on his face, sending a shock of recognition through her.

'You don't have to say yes if you'd rather not,' he said

huskily, so softly that she could hardly hear him. 'It's just that you've been driving me crazy ever since that last night at my cottage. I haven't been able to get you out of my mind.'

'I…' she managed to get out. 'Um…it would depend on what I'd be saying yes to.' Trying to turn it into a joke, she smiled. But an air of seriousness seemed to hang between them.

'I'm not looking for an affair. I know you'll be gone soon…' he said.

'Why me?' she whispered.

'Because you've somehow got through my defences, I guess,' he said. 'Also, you're a lovely woman, of course.'

Signy swallowed nervously then put up her hand to his face, without having planned it. Her eyes moved from his eyes to his mouth. God help me, she said to herself, I don't know what I'm doing. With that, she leaned forward the few inches and put her mouth tentatively on his by way of answer, the contact melting any residual resistance. A feeling of intense longing flared through her.

Immediately his mouth captured hers hungrily, urgently, his hands on either side of her face, straining her to him as though he had been waiting for ever for this, she thought wildly. Any man could do this to me now, and I would respond in the same way. Stubbornly she denied any special power to Dan. I've been waiting for this, too…

Dan cradled her in his arms, his kiss deepening, and she found herself responding mindlessly, carried along with his passion. In moments her hands had moved up to his hair, which was surprisingly soft and fine.

They lay down on the ground next to each other, their heads on the soft, dry earth which was scented with the pungent odour of growing things. To Signy, being there with Dan began to take on that rare magical quality that the mist, the sea and the forest brought with them, as though he were very much a part of it all. Like the inconstant mist, perhaps he, too, would disappear…as he surely would for her when she left this island.

Now all that mattered was the feel of his warm mouth on hers, his head above hers, his hands caressing her face as he kissed her. All her reservations were temporarily forgotten. It had been a long time since a man had wanted her in this way, or since she had felt herself respond with such hunger. The time she had spent with Simon now seemed like a gauche dress-rehearsal for a more intense, mature coming of age. Whether it was to be with this man, she didn't know.

Short and sweet, that was what Terri had suggested, she reminded herself wildly. Was this to be it? With this strange man whom she didn't understand?

They pulled apart and lay looking at each other, breathing quickly. Looking up at him, she felt shy, especially when he stroked strands of hair away from her forehead. There was something very disarming about gentleness in a man who was what one might call a man of action.

'I didn't come for this, Signy,' he said softly, the expression in his eyes gentle yet unreadable. 'You must believe that. I wanted to talk to you, to make sure you were all right.'

'I know,' she said. It was true.

'Signy…you're very lovely,' he murmured, 'in more ways than one. Never be tempted to sell yourself short.' The implied finality in his words meant that they were ships that were destined to pass in the night. It seemed so, anyway. An odd feeling, presaging future goodbyes, moved her to the brink of tears, so that she had to blink rapidly to forestall the threatened moisture. Not that he meant anything to her. He was just kind, and she appreciated that. She was more emotionally labile than she had thought.

'We're ships that pass in the night, aren't we?' She put her thought into words, trying to be flippant.

'It would seem so,' he said, looking down at her.

When he bent to kiss her again, she put her arms up around his neck, a feeling of finality, of those future good-byes, goading her to make the most of this man-woman contact. It was nice, she told herself, to be held, to be kissed…especially when you read passion and desire in a man's eyes…

The rain did slacken off, just as Dan had predicted. They walked back quickly along the path, where here and there small puddles had collected. For the rest of her life she would remember that walk, she knew, because there would never be anything quite like it again. In hot, dry places she would think of the dark green, moist coolness, the scents of cedar and rich black soil, the glimpses of pale sky far above where the branches of the towering trees met, the light of a weak sun shafting through.

When they were at the edge of the camp, Dan turned to her on the path. 'You managed not to talk to me about yourself, Signy Clover,' he teased. 'You were too intent on getting my story.'

It was her turn to shrug now. 'You can't have it all your way,' she said. 'And I suspect that I didn't get very much of your story. Well, Dan…goodbye.'

'Goodbye. Remember, I'm around if you need me,' he said.

They parted there, and went their separate ways.

CHAPTER EIGHT

THE next days and then weeks seemed to go by with amazing rapidity. Time was filled with lectures, training sessions, shooting practice, seminar discussions, reading the required texts and making copious and comprehensive notes about everything. In between all this, they learned how to cope with the wilderness, as well as how to be of help in the local communities.

With immense satisfaction, Signy saw her file of notes becoming fatter by the day and knew that once she got back to England she would go over this stuff and fully realize its tremendous value. Then she would organize it all to bring it to a more formal order. She was sure that one day, on her next assignment, she would be able to put it to good use in the field.

Thinking ahead to being back in England at her parents' pleasant country house, her childhood home, she had both a feeling of homesickness and a very strange prescient sense of missing Kelp Island, the people she had met there, the friends she had made and was making. Yes, she would miss it all. Knowing that it was a unique experience, she determined to make the most of every single moment of her time. Accordingly, she and all the others went for frequent walks, explored the island, enjoyed just being in the camp.

The weather was changing as the year passed relentlessly towards winter. There was much more heavy rain, more mists and fog.

'Have you changed your mind about not going home

for Christmas, Signy?' Terri said to her one day. 'I hope you haven't, because I sure can't afford to go back to Australia for a week, then come back here for two weeks or so just before this course ends. Besides, I'd be knackered by the journey. I wouldn't want to be here without you. Connie's going home, and Pearl's staying here, too.'

'No, I'm not going back,' Signy confirmed. 'We can all have fun together in that Vancouver hotel that's been booked for us downtown. We can sing carols, do some shopping, do a round of the cafés for *caffelatte*, drink wine... Ah, I can just picture it. A touch of luxury.'

'Yep,' Terri sighed, a far-away look in her eyes, 'I'm really going to enjoy it.'

Since her walk through the woods with Dan, all Signy's interaction with him had been in the company of other people. Oddly enough, she was beginning to find this frustrating as she was feeling the need to talk to him at last. Sometimes she felt that he was deliberately keeping it that way, forcing her gently into a position where she would have to make a move, to come to him if she wanted help. After all, she told herself realistically, he had offered frequently enough, so now it was really up to her to seize the moment, if that was what she really wanted.

Several times they went back to Brookes Landing, and other places inland, north of Vancouver, along the coast, to which they could travel by float plane and Land Rover. Signy found herself mostly in the company of Terri, Connie and Pearl. Sometimes Dan or Max was with them, sometimes a local nurse. The remaining time began to seem very precious.

Finding herself in Brookes Landing Hospital one day in late November, Signy and Connie decided that they would like to visit Felix George again as they had some free time. Since the first meeting they had seen him again, twice, but knew that there wouldn't be many more opportunities.

'Let's ask Dan if we can go there without him,' Connie suggested.

'Yes. I'd like to see his wife, too. I really admire how she's coping with him, with everything,' Signy said. 'We could, perhaps, take one of the hospital vans—it won't be for long.'

'Right. Let's see if we can find Dan,' Connie said. 'I heard earlier that he was in the OR.'

As they made their way to the OR, intending to go to the small recreation room there where the doctors and nurses took their brief coffee- and tea-breaks, Signy found that she was looking forward to seeing Dan. Since they'd kissed and been more intimate, she'd found her attitude to him changing, perhaps inevitably, to feel that she had somehow a proprietorial interest in him. Perversely, she almost resented what she now saw as his withdrawal from her into work.

Of course, it had been inadvertent that they'd been thrown together when she'd been forced to be a guest at his cottage, she mused as she and Connie walked the hospital corridors. Knowing it to be inappropriate, as she would soon be away from here, she fought against it. Nonetheless, it assailed her again, a sense of muted excitement. Perhaps the sooner she was away from here, the better…even though she would miss it and be haunted by the beauty of the place, the people she'd met. There would have to be a necessary emotional disengagement.

Dan came into the coffee-room after they'd been there a few minutes. To Signy, he looked shockingly exhausted. If they'd been alone she would have asked him what he'd been doing; as it was, they just talked about Felix George.

'I'm sure they would like a visit, particularly Donna,' he said. 'She feels pretty isolated at times, although she has friends who take her out and give her breaks. You'll see a change in Felix, unfortunately.'

'Could we borrow a van from the hospital?' Signy asked. 'We won't stay out more than an hour.'

'Take my Land Rover,' he offered, looking at her consideringly. They might never have been in each other's arms, she thought.

'That's kind of you,' she said. 'Thank you.'

As time was of the essence, she and Connie found the vehicle and were on the road within five minutes, with Signy driving and Connie looking over the map. On the way, Connie gave Donna a call on her cellphone to let her know they were coming.

'Is there anything we can bring you?' she offered. 'We haven't gone by the last store yet.'

Connie jerked her thumb in the direction of the last grocery store on the road before the edge of the village, so that Signy knew to veer off there. 'Will do,' she said to Donna. Then she turned to Signy: 'Donna could use a few groceries.'

When they approached the George house some time later carrying the groceries, Donna opened the front door and came out.

'It's so great to see you,' she said smiling, 'and thank you so much for those groceries. Come in. Felix is sleeping, and I don't want to wake him. We'll go into the kitchen and have tea and cake. There are things I want to discuss with you…ask you about.'

'OK, Donna,' Connie said. 'Lead the way.' They spoke quietly so as not to disturb Felix.

When the electric kettle was plugged in and Donna had closed the kitchen door quietly, she turned to the two nurses. 'Felix isn't too good,' she began. 'Last night we were talking things over, and he has come round to the idea—and I agree—that he should try another course of chemotherapy. At one point he said he never wanted any more, it made him feel so bad. But now…he's feeling not too good anyway, so he maybe figured he might as well try the other stuff again.'

Both nurses nodded in commiseration. 'Would that mean going to Vancouver to a teaching hospital?' Signy said, her heart going out to this woman who was struggling to do the right thing by her husband.

'Yes. I would go with him, of course. Dr Blake has a place there for patients from Brookes Landing, so he lets us stay there.'

'Does Dr Blake know that you've decided this?' Signy went on, as Dan hadn't mentioned it.

'No…we just decided last night, Felix and I,' Donna said. 'I know that Dr Blake will go along with what we want. I thank God every day that we've got him for our doctor. I don't think you could have a better one anywhere in the world.' Her voice shook as she spoke, and Signy wanted to put her arms around her.

'Would you like us to tell him what you've decided?' Connie offered. 'He knows we're here.'

'Would you? That would be great,' Donna said, distracting herself by getting the tea ready.

When they had drunk two cups of tea and talked a lot about issues that needed to be discussed, Connie stood up. 'We have to get back now, Donna, because we've got Dr Blake's car. Could we just have a peep at Felix? Just so that we can tell Dan that we've seen him. We'll be careful not to wake him.'

The three of them crept into the den that Felix used as

his sanctuary. On the narrow day-bed he was lying on his side with a blanket covering him.

Indeed, there was a change in him, Signy thought sadly as she looked at his gaunt face, which had an unhealthy yellowish pallor. They stood there for a few moments, then silently went out of the room.

On the doorstep, saying goodbye, Signy took a good look around, knowing that she might never come back here again. 'This is such a lovely spot,' she said to Donna.

'You should see it in the summer,' Donna said. 'Such lovely wild flowers. You can get a great view up that way.' She gestured back down the track. 'Back to the main track, then on a bit, then a little way to the right down a narrow track... You can just get a car down there—there's a look-out tower for fire-spotting. Used to be used a lot in the old days. It's still used, but now people can go up in planes. You can climb up there on a clear day and see a long way around. Very peaceful and lovely it is.'

'Maybe we'll go there some time,' Connie said.

'Don't walk up there,' Donna said warningly. 'It's a bit of a wild place and there might be cougars or bears, so go by car and park right at the base, then you can climb up the steps. There's a tiny hut at the top for shelter. You can see right over the tops of the trees and down to the harbour on one side.'

On the drive back to town, with Connie driving this time, they said very little, saddened by the obvious deterioration of Dan's patient.

'Could you tell Dan, Signy?' Connie asked while she was parking the Land Rover. 'I want to lie down a bit to sleep.'

'Yes, all right,' Signy said, taking the vehicle keys from Connie, thinking that maybe Connie didn't want to dwell any more on the case of Felix, possibly wanted to shed a few tears. 'I expect I'll see you later in the dining room.'

Dan was just coming out of the OR suite when Signy got there.

'Hi, Signy,' he said with a slight, tired smile as he shrugged into a white lab coat over his scrub suit. 'I assume you're back from having seen Felix? How was he?'

'Here are your keys,' she said, handing them to him. 'Thank you for the use of the car. Um…as you said, Felix has deteriorated…at least, since I saw him last. He was actually asleep. He and his wife have decided that he should go for another course of chemotherapy if you're in agreement. They asked me to pass on the message.'

Dan stepped aside, taking her arm, as other people came out of the OR.

'We're in the way here,' he said, pulling her to one side. 'Look, I'm just on my way to the dining room for a quick break. Come with me, and you can tell me what Donna said.' He ran a hand through his hair tiredly.

'All right.' Signy nodded. 'I could use something to eat.' A feeling of compassion for him came over her. Obviously he worked extremely hard, was almost constantly on call while he was in Brookes Landing, put his patients' interests first and foremost. Also, she was pleased to be with him…

'I've got Kathy Lahey in labour,' he said as they walked. 'She just came in this morning, so I have to be around for that. At the moment she's doing well.'

'It's a little early, I think, isn't it?' Signy asked.

'Yes, but it won't matter, the baby's a good size.'

When they were seated in the dining room, she told him what Donna had said.

'I'll make a few phone calls to the city,' he said pensively. 'Get it arranged from that end, for him to see an oncologist for reassessment. I fear it's too late for more chemotherapy—it probably wouldn't do any good…it would just make him feel rotten at a time when he couldn't cope with it. The sooner we can get him there, the better. I'll call Donna, then see if I can get up to visit him later today…or one of the nurses will.'

They ate in silence for a while. 'Well, Signy,' he said, looking at her astutely. 'How are you these days? We haven't really seen much of each other.'

The intent regard made her acutely aware of him. She was pleased to see him, to be the focus of his attention, if only for a brief interlude. Odd, that.

'Actually, I'm all right, thanks,' she said, trying not to give him any hint of what was passing through her mind. 'I'm feeling the benefit of being here now. I'm more relaxed, learning new things. Really, it's been very good for me.'

'Mmm,' he said, smiling slightly. 'I assume you've got a room here at the hospital for the week?'

'Yes.'

They continued to talk while they ate, surrounded by the steady comings and going of other staff. Signy exchanged a few words with Pearl and Terri as they were passing through. There was a pleasant atmosphere in this place, she thought. The people here were friendly and dedicated to their jobs, with a strong sense of teamwork. Many small places didn't attract the best people, or even those who were good, yet this place seemed to be very fortunate that it had Dan and Max on the medical staff, plus some very good registered nurses.

'I'd better get back,' Dan said, glancing at the clock. 'I've got two other women in labour, and I've just done a Caesarean section. One of those days.' He leaned forward. 'Perhaps you'd come out for a drink with me one evening, Signy? I guess you've been to the pub here?'

'Hank's Emporium?' She laughed. 'I went in there once.'

'Mmm.' He smiled back. 'It used to be a sort of trading post-cum-general store, that sold alcohol as well on the side. Now it's legit.'

'I'd like to,' she said.

'Right,' he said, standing up. 'I'll keep you to that.' With a quick squeeze of her shoulder, he left her.

That gesture, it seemed to her, was a slight acknowledgement that he was thinking of how he had held her in his arms and kissed her under the tree in a rainstorm. How odd life was, she mused, that you were sometimes thrown together with someone you essentially felt was alien to you, then against your will you found yourself seeing them in a totally different light. As she watched him move away from her, Signy had a sobering feeling that they would never go to Hank's Emporium together. Most likely, he would be too busy.

Her afternoon was free so, like Connie, she would take advantage of the break to have a much-needed sleep in the tiny utilitarian room that had been assigned to her in the staff quarters.

Something woke Signy in the night. One moment she was fast asleep, not dreaming, then her eyelids sprang open and she found herself staring at the dark ceiling, totally alert.

The job she did had taught her to be ready for any emergency—to have a pair of appropriate shoes or boots near the bed, a set of suitable clothing on a chair within reach, with a coat or jacket, to have her vital papers in a small knapsack close to hand, so that if she had to flee or take action she could be out of a room in a very short time. Now she did a lightning mental inventory of exactly where everything was placed.

Chink, chink, chink, chink... A sharp, tinny sound came from inside the room. As she lay there, it took her only seconds to realize what was happening, and a sense of fear, coupled with something like wonder, caused a sudden surge of adrenalin through her body. She had often read that intense fear had a paralysing effect, the fear of imminent physical danger. In Africa she had experienced that. The few seconds of wakefulness seemed like long moments, suspended in time.

The sound came from bottles and other objects knocking together on the small, narrow table in the room that served as a dressing-table. At the same time, she had a sense that the bed was moving very slightly.

Quickly she leaned over to put on the bedside light, then swung out of bed and pulled on clothes and hiking boots. 'Oh, God,' she whispered. This must be an earth tremor, she concluded. If it had been an earthquake, there would be something more. Already the shaking had stopped, as far as she could tell. Grabbing her knapsack, she went into the passage. Doors were opening, other nurses emerging, some dressed, some in their night-clothes.

'Was that an earth tremor?' Signy asked one of the others, whom she hadn't met before.

'I think so,' the other young woman said, looking scared. 'Something woke me up, then the bed began to shake. It seems to be over now.'

'What was that?' Terri asked as she emerged, partially dressed, carrying her shoes.

'A tremor, we think,' Signy said.

'We'd better get over to the rallying point, which is the

lobby for us in this part of the hospital,' the other nurse said. 'That's the emergency procedure. Even if it's all over, we should still report there to be briefed.'

As she waited for Terri to finish dressing hastily, she considered the emergency protocol. As the four World Aid nurses weren't part of the permanent staff, they would wait for instructions with regard to duties. This time there seemed to be a reprieve.

The four WAN nurses arrived in the main lobby to find quite a crowd of staff there, including Dan and Max, plus the night supervisor—a nurse—of the hospital.

'You all OK?' Dan asked the nurses, having pushed his way over to them.

'We're fine,' Pearl answered. 'Just as scared as hell.'

'It seems to be over, although there are sometimes a few after-shocks,' Dan said. 'If they come, they should be pretty mild.'

'Thank God for that,' Terri said.

The supervisor stood up on a bench and started to speak, so the chatter of the crowd stopped. Dan moved to stand next to Signy. 'You OK?' He mouthed the words.

She nodded, swallowing a tight knot of fear in her throat. Usually one could rely on the integrity of the soil beneath one's feet. Dan looked even more exhausted than he had when she'd last seen him. It appeared that he was still up, working, perhaps delivering babies.

'What you felt,' the supervisor said, getting right to the point, 'was an earth tremor that resulted from a earthquake out at sea, with the epicentre about one hundred and fifty kilometres beyond the islands. We got that information a moment or two ago from the monitoring station. There shouldn't be anything more happening, but I ask you to remain in your rooms, fully clothed and alert, for the next half-hour at least, just to remain ready. I commend you on your swift response in mustering at this point. For those of you who are new here, please read the printed emergency procedures in your rooms. For those who are on duty, make sure your whereabouts are known to your colleagues at all times. Stay in your departments. Check your emergency equipment. That's all for now.'

When she had gone, chatter broke out, with an exchange of information about what everyone had experienced.

'Is that enough excitement for you with regard to earthquakes?' Dan addressed the four WAN nurses with a wry grin.

'It is,' Pearl said emphatically. 'I think I'd rather have a hurricane.'

'Kathy Lahey gave birth to a boy, by the way,' Dan said to Connie and Signy. 'Both well.'

'That's good.' Signy smiled. 'Could I come to help you with anything? I know I won't sleep for the remainder of the night.'

'Sure,' he said. 'Anyone who wants to come is very welcome. Go to your rooms first to wait out the half-hour and read the instructions.'

'I'm glad this has happened,' Terri commented as they left the room. 'Now we'll have at least a slight idea of what people have experienced when they've been in an earthquake.'

'The fear, anyway,' Pearl said.

It was two weeks later when they were next in Brookes Landing. The weather was closing in, with fog and snow flurries. The WAN staff had been told that these few days would be their last in the community. From now on they would be doing theoretical work only, back at the camp on Kelp Island, as the weather would hamper travel, and they would take a week's break for Christmas.

A little snow had settled on some of the trees in the village, making the conifers look like Christmas trees, on the day that Signy decided to borrow a vehicle from the hospital and drive to the lookout tower that was used for fire-spotting in the event of forest fires. The sun was shining, the light glittering on the snow. Visibility was good, making it perhaps the last day to get a view over the forested areas and the wilderness beyond Brookes Landing. Accordingly, she arranged with Maggie at Reception to borrow a Land Rover to go to visit Kathy Lahey and her baby at home, then go on the tower. None of the other nurses had been free to come with her.

As she searched for the track Donna had described some time before, having visited mother and baby, Signy looked at the scene around her, knowing that this was as close as she was going to get to the real Canada, the beginning of vast territory where there were no humans, that was frequented only by wildlife. It was an exciting feeling. The vehicle bucked and swayed over rough terrain.

At the end of the track, she abruptly came out of the trees into a rough clearing, where the tower, looking like an electricity pylon, made of metal, stood in the centre. At the top was a tiny wooden hut, and there were metal steps going up to it. She drove around the base of the tower and parked the Land Rover facing the track she had just come on. She would have to watch the time to be back to Brookes Landing before dusk, as she didn't want to be driving in the dark. Besides, hunting animals came out at dusk.

The air was crisp and fresh, she noted as she stepped out into it, a few degrees colder than in Brookes Landing.

Filled with anticipation, Signy began at once to climb the tower steps that went up to small landings at every sixth step. Once she was above the level of some of the lower trees, she stopped to take her camera out of her knapsack and take photographs from several angles. The forest was spread out before her, like a lumpy blanket in several hues of green. When she got back to England she would enjoy looking at these pictures. The whole trip would seem like a dream if she didn't have concrete items to look at.

From the very top landing, which was mostly taken up by the hut, she could see the ocean in the direction from which she had come.

'Wow!' she whispered, wishing that there was someone there to share this spectacular view with her. Dan came to mind, then she tried to force thoughts of him from her...unsuccessfully. As the time drew near for the training course to end, her emotions regarding Dan were becoming increasingly ambivalent and disruptive of her equilibrium. As hard as she had tried to maintain her dislike—almost for Dominic's sake—it had slowly fizzled out until what was left was a disturbing awareness of him as a man, and of herself as a woman, a free woman. Once a man had kissed you, she thought as she looked out over the treetops, you couldn't pretend that it hadn't happened, or that it didn't mean anything. There had been no sort of follow-up, which she was finding frustrating.

Not that he thought anything special of her, she mused. He still sought her out, it seemed, still worked with her when he could, even though she sensed a certain cynicism in him, not so much with her as with male-female relationships in general. As for her, she didn't know what to do. She had both a sense of relief that the strain would soon be over, and a sense of something like dread that she would most likely never see him again. He had somehow grown on her…had, by gradual increments, broken through the barrier that she had put up.

Signy willed her emotions back to the wonderful scene in front of her and felt herself become immersed in it. The forest disappeared into the far distance, into a grey-green mist. Then she got busy again with her camera.

The hut had room for three people to stand side by side. There was a door that had a sturdy latch on it, and a double-glazed picture window facing away from Brookes Landing. This was one of the most spectacular and moving things she had seen in her life, even though she felt insignificant surrounded by raw nature. The vehicle and her cellphone were her links to the world where she had some control against that nature.

Absorbed with taking photographs, at the end of her second roll of film, Signy realized that the light was fading, bringing an added chill. Quickly packing up her camera, she turned to go down the steps. Not very happy with heights, she tried not to look down for more than the next six steps, to the next landing, until she was more than halfway down the tower and the distance to go didn't seem too intimidating.

'Ah…' She let out a sigh of contentment, taking one more slow look around her in all directions before she sank below the tops of the shorter trees.

Risking a look down to the clearing directly below, which was covered with rough grass and tiny bushes, she froze as she saw movement by the Land Rover. With one hand she gripped the outer metal railing beside the steps and peered down. For a moment she could see nothing moving, then something took shape, the same colour as the brownish-yellow grass. Beside the wheel of the Land Rover a large cat sniffed at the tyre, then moved sinuously to sniff at the door which she'd left unlatched, open about a quarter of an inch.

A feeling of shock came over her like a sickness, paralysing her, together with a certainty that this was a cougar. As she stared down onto its tawny back and head, it suddenly looked up at her and crouched down slightly. Perhaps she had made a slight sound, an intake of breath. Its eyes looked directly into hers, a look from predator to prey. Never in her life had Signy seen such a look of cold intent in the eyes of a creature as it held itself immobile, staring at her.

Gripping the rail tightly, Signy began to climb backwards up the stairs, wondering frantically if cougars could climb stairs. She didn't see why they couldn't. Not wanting to take her eyes off it, her progress was sickeningly slow. If she could make it to the top she could shut herself in the hut. She couldn't risk going down to the vehicle. As she moved she made plans. Perhaps she would have to stay in the hut all night. Cougars hunted mainly at night and it was coming up to dusk now. Thank heaven she had a cellphone on her, plus some food and drink and warm clothes. The nights were cold now as soon as the sun began to go down. She berated herself for not leaving sooner.

As she slowly gained the upper levels, the big cat moved to a spot under the centre of the tower to look up at her. Then she didn't doubt that it could climb steps…but whether it would actually do so was another matter. At two landings from the top, she turned and ran up to the hut, yanked open the door and went inside. Her hands shook as she latched the door shut with the sturdy metal hasp. In the floor of the hut was a tiny trapdoor through which she could see the base of the tower. As she looked down, the cougar looked up, although she doubted whether it could see her clearly.

Signy sat down on the floor and leaned back against the wall, trying to think about the best course of action. There was no way she could go down and drive away now. Even if the cougar went into the forest, it would probably lie in wait for her. No…there was nothing for it but to wait there all night, then make a dash for the vehicle when the sun was well up. It would be cold; already she felt somewhat chilled.

From her knapsack she took her cellphone and small address book and looked for the number of Terri's cellphone. Several people knew where she had gone. She didn't expect anyone to come and rescue her, she simply wanted to let them know where she was, and safe.

'Terri Carpenter,' the bright voice answered, after she had punched in Terri's number. It had been a while—when she'd been in Africa—since Signy had felt such abject relief.

'Terri, it's Signy,' she said. 'I'm stuck up in a tower, being held hostage by a cougar.'

'Well, if you ain't joking,' Terri said after a moment's stunned silence, 'that's a beaut!'

The sound of a vehicle, far below, penetrated Signy's fuzzy mind as she allowed herself to doze but not fall asleep. Outside there was total darkness and a wind that buffeted her small sanctuary from time to time. She sat on the floor of the hut with her knees drawn up, her arms around her knees, her head on her arms, leaning against the wall. Although the walls were sturdy, the cold penetrated the structure. Before bedding down for the night, she had put on every item of clothing that she'd brought with her, including hat and gloves.

When she looked through the hatch she saw the light

from headlamps showing up the base of the tower in sharp relief against the dark forest. To her surprise, there was a thin blanket of snow on the ground, while some flakes still fell, showing up like sparklers in the lights of the car. Not knowing whether this was someone who had come to find her, she waited with her heart beating fast. Until she knew who was there, she didn't want to reveal herself. Silently she watched as two men got out of an all-terrain vehicle, leaving the lights on. They both carried shotguns. One of them walked over to her Land Rover and put on the headlights, then he looked up. She saw that it was Dan.

Relief suffused her being like a warm wave. 'Thank God!' she whispered. 'Thank you, Dan.' Terri must have let Dan know where she was, although she had told Terri that she would come out in the morning.

Then he began to climb the stairs, carrying a flashlight, so she went to the door and shouted down to him. Although she had been prepared to stay there all night, knowing that she shouldn't have waited until the light had begun to fade, she would rather get out. The sick feeling of fear, which had been with her from the moment she'd spotted the cougar, lessened with every step that Dan took towards her.

'Stay there until I reach you,' he shouted back.

She stood in the open doorway of the hut, then stepped back when he made the final landing, momentarily blinded when he shone the flashlight at her.

'Well, Signy Clover,' he said, ducking through the doorway, 'I suspected that you would be trouble when I first set eyes on you.'

'Th-thank you for coming,' she said, her teeth chattering now from cold. 'I didn't mean to get you out here. I was quite prepared to stay here for the night. I told Terri that.'

'And freeze to death in the process?' he said.

With that, he pulled her roughly into his arms and kissed her. 'I didn't call you,' he said, 'because I suspected you would refuse to be rescued—pig-headed as you are.'

'Pig-headed!' she began to protest, but he kissed her again, holding her against him in a bear hug.

'Shut up,' he said. Abruptly he let her go. 'I've got one of the hospital security guys with me. He's more concerned about the hospital vehicle than he is about you, so he's going to drive that one back. You can come with me.' The way he said it sounded like a threat.

Silently Signy picked up her gear, stuffing the flashlight into the knapsack.

'Come on,' Dan said, taking her hand. 'Let's get out of here.'

With his light making a circle of yellow ahead of them, they descended the stairs. At the bottom, he introduced her to the security guard, who simply said, 'Hi. I'm glad you're safe. You don't mess with cougars.'

The track and then the road going back to Brookes Landing were covered with a light snow, making everything look different. On the outskirts of the village the security guard veered off towards the hospital while Dan took another road.

'I'm taking you to Heron Cottage,' Dan said. 'You need to get heated up pretty quickly. You should have a bath and a hot drink right away.' His face looked grim, and in the light from the streetlamps Signy could see that he looked more than exhausted, he looked haggard.

She said nothing, shivering with cold now, even though he had given her a thick wool blanket to wrap around herself. Deeply sorry that he'd been bothered, she felt sheepish in the extreme. It seemed that she was always in the wrong with him somehow.

Inside Heron Cottage at last, he told her to sit by the fire while he ran a bath for her.

'I can do it…Dan,' she protested. 'Thank you for what you've done. I'm truly and deeply grateful, but I can look after myself.'

'Shut up,' he said grimly. 'Don't overdo the thanks. And do what you're told for once. Someone in Africa should have told you the same thing. You don't know this terrain. I do.'

'I know the way to the bathroom,' she said tartly.

'Shut up.' At that moment he sounded very English. Perhaps in moments of extreme stress he reverted to his roots. That observation made her realize fully that he had been seriously worried about her.

'I'm so sorry.' Signy sank down on the rug next to the fire, where the embers glowed red and hot, pulling the blanket around her.

'So you ought to be!' He almost spat the words at her. His anger didn't faze her; in fact, she felt uncommonly cosseted and loved, like a lost child who had been found.

Loved? She didn't want to dwell on that. Now that she was back here, in the cosy warmth, the full enormity of her situation hit her. She'd had a lucky escape once again. Perhaps, like a cat, she had nine lives. With eyes closed, she tried to relax in the blessed heat as she heard the sound of bath water running in the guest room, then Dan clattering about in the kitchen with a certain amount of unnecessary banging.

'Get into the bath,' he ordered her, after a few minutes. 'I'll make us both a hot drink, something with brandy.'

Not trusting herself to speak, she did as he told her. Best to humour him, she thought, feeling his anger with her, even though she thought she had been on top of the situation. She sank down into the hot water so that only her head was out of it, feeling the heat infuse her body, chilled to the bone as she was.

When a knock came on the door she was pleasantly warm, her cheeks glowing. Quickly she scrambled out of the bath and wrapped herself in the voluminous towel that Dan had given her. 'Come in.'

With another peremptory knock, Dan came in and handed her a mug of steaming liquid. 'Drink this right away,' he ordered again, his eyes going over her swiftly, down to her bare feet.

'Thank you, Dan,' she mumbled. 'I'm really sorry for all this.'

'All in a day's work,' he said brusquely. 'I'll bring you something to put on. Don't apologize again.'

'It's all…' she began, but he was gone. Resignedly, bemused, Signy dried herself.

Again he entered, with pyjamas, a dressing-gown and woolly socks. 'Come and sit by the fire when you're ready,' he said. 'We'll have some soup. I guess you haven't eaten for a while.'

'No.'

The drink he'd brought her was hot milk with honey and brandy, so delicious and soothing that she sipped it slowly to make it last. When she was dressed in the clothes he had brought, she felt like a child in dressing-up clothes and had to roll up the sleeves and legs of the pyjamas.

The fire was roaring when she went out to sit beside it. True to his word, Dan brought her soup, which he placed on a small coffee-table that he drew up to the fireplace, a bowl for each of them. To her embarrassment, Signy found that she couldn't think of anything to say to him, except a small 'thank you' when he handed her something, even though thoughts and emotions seemed to be buzzing around inside her head like so many angry bees.

There was so much she wanted to say to him, yet she could not think where to begin, how to make a start.

Methodically, he cleared away the used dishes when they had finished and rearranged the furniture, while Signy sat down on the floor by the fire again, brooding over what might have happened to her if she hadn't seen the cougar in the clearing, if it had been lurking among the trees and had attacked her while she'd gone to get into her car.

Dan came and knelt down beside her. 'Feeling OK?' he said. So tired did he look that she wanted to touch his face, to say again that she was sorry. Am I the cause of that? she asked herself. No...doubt it, she answered herself.

'A thousand times better. Thank you again, Dan, for everything,' she said, her voice coming out husky and stilted to her own ears. 'I expect you'll be very happy to see the last of the WAN group, won't you? Especially me. You look so tired...'

'Does that make up for the death of Dominic Fraser, in your estimation?' he said, a cynical note in his voice, his mouth twisted in that wry way that he had.

'I...I know you didn't do anything wrong there,' she said. 'I've more or less come to terms with that.'

'Only more or less?' he said, the cynical note more pronounced. 'Perhaps I can do something about that.'

When he leaned forward and kissed her, she wasn't prepared for it. Hot from the bath and the fire, she nonetheless felt an additional flare of heat as she responded to him, closing her eyes to let the feel of his mouth on hers fill her whole being with delightful sensation. Coupled with the sense of relief at being safe, it was a powerful combination.

'Oh, Dan...' she whispered, wanting to weep as they separated, putting her hand up to touch his neck. Without premeditation, she lay back on the floor in the orange glow and heat from the fire, closing her eyes. Now that she was safe, a terrible weariness came with letting go. 'Please, hold me,' she added brokenly.

It seemed that all her past and present angst was coming together in that moment, and all she wanted in the world was for Dan to hold her in his arms. Instead of him feeling alien to her, they seemed for the moment powerfully two of a kind, and joined in a bond by the work they did. In his person he seemed dear and familiar, as well as exciting and very, very attractive...

When he kissed her fiercely, holding her to him as they lay side by side, she put her arms around him and clung on as though she were drowning, kissing him back hungrily. Wanting something for herself, she also wanted to erase that abject exhaustion from his face.

Dan sat up and pulled her up beside him, his arm around her shoulders, and stared into the fire. By putting his hand on the side of her face, he eased her head down to rest on his shoulder, where she could feel the beating of his heart and the uneven pace of his breathing. They were both, it seemed to her, struggling for control, on the brink of something momentous.

'Are you ready to talk to me?' he said, after a few minutes. 'Because, if you are, I want to hear all about Simon Heathcote. There's plenty of time, because I have the day off tomorrow.'

Signy began to talk then, pouring out her heart to him, the sentences tumbling out as though they had already formed long ago in her mind and had just been waiting for her to open the flood-gates. She told him about her life in London, her work there, when she had been all unaware about other, broader aspects of life. She told him about her family, her mother and two brothers, her father who was a GP in a small English town and wanted to retire soon because he was chronically tired. There was Simon, about whom she could suddenly be objective, then there was Africa and WAN.

By the time she fell silent they were holding each other in a close embrace. It was a companionable silence, yet filled with vivid undercurrents of emotion which they left undisturbed for some time while his hand idly toyed with her hair, sensitizing her unbearably to his touch. Signy knew that everything had suddenly, decisively shifted and changed, so that the time in her life when she hadn't known that Dan Blake existed seemed to recede from her.

Dan tilted her face up to his, holding her chin, while he looked deeply into her eyes. 'You have three choices, Signy Clover,' he said, his face serious as his eyes darkened. 'You can sleep on the sofa here, you can sleep in the spare bedroom…or you can sleep with me.' Then he gave her that slight, slow smile that she found she could no longer resist.

'I…don't want to be alone.' she whispered.

'I'll give you one more chance to back out,' he said huskily. 'My intention is to stay in bed all day tomorrow, not to answer the phone, to be out to everyone but you. And I shall expect you to stay with me.'

Smiling back, she finally acknowledged what she had been fighting for a long time. She was in love with Dr Dan Blake, and the thought of never seeing him again after next month was unbearable, against the natural order of things. In reply, she kissed him, matching his passion with hers, tremulous and hopeful.

'Is there some way,' he asked, his lips against hers, 'that we can spend time together after this course ends?'

'We can always find a way,' she murmured, an absurd happiness filling her whole being.

'I love you, so help me,' Dan said, nuzzling his cheek

against hers. 'I didn't want to admit it before… It complicates things.'

'Oh…' she said. 'Oh…'

'Is that all you can say?' he teased.

'I love you, too,' she whispered. 'Crazy, isn't it?'

'Yes…and no,' he said. 'Will you spend some of the Christmas holiday with me in the city? I know you want to keep the others company some of the time. Make time for me. Please.'

They smiled at each other, their eyes alight with love. 'Let's go to bed first,' Signy teased. 'Then I'll give you my answer.'

'Testing me out?' He laughed, the action erasing some of the tiredness in his face, and Signy felt herself melting, all resistance gone. This wonderful man, a mature man of integrity, humility, compassion, intelligence, dedication, empathy…all the positive qualities she had always been looking for, if unconsciously, in a man…actually wanted to be with her. Moreover, he was a man she found almost unbearably attractive, the broken nose the sexiest thing she had ever seen.

'If you like,' she said, laughing back.

'I do like.' He pulled her up, then swung her up into his arms to carry her.

In his bedroom it took him only moments to take off the oversized dressing-gown, pyjamas and finally the woolly socks that she was wearing, to hold back the thick duvet on his bed for her to get under. While he undressed, she watched him, knowing that at last she had grown up.

As she held her arms open to him and he came into them, she whispered, 'About Christmas…yes.'

'And after?' he murmured, holding her against the length of his body, so that shivers of pleasure coursed through her.

'Will there be an ''after'', Dan?' she murmured against

his neck, as he ran a hand warmly along her side, smoothing his palm over her breast.

'I hope so, Signy…I hope so.'

In the morning he brought her tea in bed. 'You spoil me, Dan.' She smiled shyly as she took it, having put on the oversized pyjama jacket again.

He sat down on the edge of the bed and looked at her, holding his own mug of tea. That awful tiredness had been erased from his face. He looked rested, his eyes alight with what Signy knew was love. The knowledge brought her humility and a certain amazement, because it seemed like a miracle when the person you loved also loved you. Instinctively she knew that his love had no strings attached, that it wouldn't be a temporary, adolescent love, but an enduring, thoughtful, passionate love. The night they had just spent together proved it.

'I have ulterior motives,' he said lightly, not taking his eyes off her.

'Oh?' she said, loving him desperately.

'There's a job going in Jamaica soon with World Aid Doctors,' he said, still looking at her as though he feared she might disappear if he didn't keep a close eye on her. The thought made Signy smile. 'They actually want two people, either two doctors or a doctor and a nurse, to set up a clinic. They've asked me if I would be interested.'

'Oh. Are you?' She kissed him, smoothing a hand over the skin of his back, confident in his love for her, and hers for him, yet not knowing what was coming. If all the other experiences had brought her to this, it was worth all the angst. 'What about your work here?'

'I have to wind it down when I go away. There are others who will take over, the other partners. I can work here or in England…and with World Aid Doctors. There will always be a place for me here,' he said. 'Of course,

I wouldn't go until Felix had finished his new course of treatment, or whatever he and Donna decide to do. I wouldn't desert him.'

'Will you go to Jamaica?' she asked. 'Away from me?' The thought was unbearable. 'I…expect I'll be back in England.'

'They'd prefer a married couple,' he said softly. 'Would you consider that, Signy Clover?'

'Oh, Dan…' she murmured.

He waited tensely.

'Did they really ask for a married couple?' she said softly, looking at him sideways. 'That…um…doesn't quite ring true, Dan.'

'No, they didn't say that,' he agreed. 'I'm not sure of you, don't want to take you for granted.' He leaned back, supporting himself on one elbow, and cupped her cheek in one hand, looking at her intently, holding her attention with his mesmerizing eyes. 'Will you marry me? With all my heart and soul I love you. More than anything I have ever wanted, or am likely to want, I want you with me for the rest of my life. Please.'

Tears pricked her eyes. 'Dan…yes…yes.'

They lay entwined in the warmth, awed and humbled in the knowledge that these were the first moments of their shared, committed life. Signy listened to rain pelting on the cedar roof, loving it because it made her feel all the more secure in Dan's arms. Sometimes miracles did happen, she mused, feeling drugged with happiness. Love could come in the most unlikely places.

Modern Romance™
...seduction and
passion guaranteed

Tender Romance™
...love affairs that
last a lifetime

Sensual Romance™
...sassy, sexy and
seductive

Blaze™
...sultry days and
steamy nights

Medical Romance™
...medical drama on
the pulse

Historical Romance™
...rich, vivid and
passionate

27 new titles every month.

*With all kinds of Romance for
every kind of mood...*

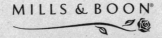

MILLS & BOON®

heat *of the* night

LORI FOSTER

GINA WILKINS

VICKI LEWIS THOMPSON

3 SIZZLING SUMMER NOVELS IN ONE

On sale 17th May 2002

Available at most branches of WH Smith,
Tesco, Martins, Borders, Eason, Sainsbury's
and most good paperback bookshops.

2 BOOKS
AND A SURPRISE GIFT!

We would like to take this opportunity to thank you for reading this Mills & Boon® book by offering you the chance to take TWO more specially selected titles from the Medical Romance™ series absolutely FREE! We're also making this offer to introduce you to the benefits of the Reader Service™—

- ★ FREE home delivery
- ★ FREE monthly Newsletter
- ★ FREE gifts and competitions
- ★ Exclusive Reader Service discount
- ★ Books available before they're in the shops

Accepting these FREE books and gift places you under no obligation to buy; you may cancel at any time, even after receiving your free shipment. Simply complete your details below and return the entire page to the address below. **You don't even need a stamp!**

YES! Please send me 2 free Medical Romance books and a surprise gift. I understand that unless you hear from me, I will receive 4 superb new titles every month for just £2.55 each, postage and packing free. I am under no obligation to purchase any books and may cancel my subscription at any time. The free books and gift will be mine to keep in any case.

M2ZEC

Ms/Mrs/Miss/Mr ....Initials ....
                                                                                BLOCK CAPITALS PLEASE

Surname ....

Address ....

....

....Postcode ....

Send this whole page to:
UK: FREEPOST CN81, Croydon, CR9 3WZ
EIRE: PO Box 4546, Kilcock, County Kildare (stamp required)